say a/sweet prayer

jennifer rebecca

Say a Sweet Prayer

Copyright 2018 © Jennifer Rebecca

Cover Design by:
Alyssa Garcia
www.uplifting-designs.com

Editing by:
Stephanie Atienza
www.uplifting-designs.com

ISBN: 978-1-7320747-4-3

For more information about Jennifer Rebecca & her books, visit
www.jenniferrebeccaauthor.com

dedication

For Sean Always:

"I'm hard to love, hard to love,
Oh I don't make it easy,
I couldn't do it if I stood where you stood
I'm hard to love, hard to love,
You say that you need me,
I don't deserve it but I love that you love me good."

-Lee Brice

"For sin shall no longer be your master, because you
are not under the law, but under grace."

-Romans 6:14

say a/sweet prayer

prologue

raw

*P*AIN. What a stupid little word to describe what I am feeling right now—*just four fucking letters*—such a mundane word to explain the white-hot lightning rips through my torso near where my heart used to be. It sears so acutely that my breath catches in my throat.

"No!" someone screams. I think it was me. It might have been me, but I don't know.

Hands grab me from behind to stop me from closing the gap between me and the bloody body on the altar steps of my family's church. These slabs of muscle and bone and joint and tendons restrain me, holding me back from the jarring loss. But the cold truth of what has come to pass is front and center for all to see.

Anguish.

This is anguish. This severe pain. A wound licked so raw that I know it will never heal. This is a wound that will only fester and turn putrid.

"Let me go!" I wail. My voice is harsh and raw.

The words are ripped from my chest leaving a raw wound in its wake.

"No," someone says. I don't know who. I don't care either. I can't stop staring at the broken remains of someone I had loved above all else. Someone who managed to do the unthinkable, to break down my walls and invade my heart.

Before I had looked at victims and wondered why couldn't I save them? Or it should have been me. But looking at the shell of what had been as it's splayed on the plush carpet of the altar steps I know without a doubt that I would trade places in a heartbeat. If only it was my blood that was spilled and not theirs.

Grief.

If this is what grief feels like I don't want it. I want to go back to this morning when my life was normal. I had had the world at my feet, and my family was whole. I feel raw . . . *exposed* . . . I'm a wound that's been flayed open down to the bone. But it cannot be stitched or cauterized.

Maybe this is shock. I don't know. All I do know is that the world is a darker place tonight. This is not a loss that I or anyone else will get over. Not now, not ever. My name is Detective Claire Goodnite, and everything has changed.

I guess it's best we say our prayers . . .

chapter 1

beautiful

"**D**ANCE WITH ME?" Wes's husky voice sounds from behind me, echoing the words he said not too long ago on the night he asked me to marry him.

I'm standing with several of our guests, a cool glass of wine in my hand when he approaches me. Other than at dinner, we have been separated from each other this evening. After the dinner service was over, we had been pulled in different directions. And all evening, I've watched that ass prowl around the room filled with our closest friends and family who have all gathered to celebrate our engagement.

Wes was wearing a custom-tailored suit in a rich, dark gray. A far cry from his usual Fed Special, but he said for this special night he was pulling out all the stops. I guess it pays to be the only son of a prominent judge. Somewhere along the way he ditched the coat and tie and rolled up the sleeves of his aqua shirt. Between the play of muscle under his corded arms, his firm ass in those fitted slacks, and the free-flowing wine, I'm having some wayward thoughts about my husband-to-be. Judging by the smirk on his face as I turn to look back at him, he knows it too.

"So?" he asks. "What'll it be, baby?"

"Yes," I whisper feeling a little breathless.

Wes extends his hand out to me and without hesitation I take it, letting him lead me out on to the makeshift dance floor.

"You are so beautiful," he says as he wraps me in his arms and slowly sways me to the music. I can't help but feel that with this man, in this moment, everything is finally right.

"Wes," I whisper. "That's just the wine talking." I duck my head down and feel a blush steal across my cheeks. I'm still a little uncomfortable with his softer side and more romantic undertones. Ever since a fellow detective tried to murder me a few weeks ago, Wes has been extra loving and attentive.

"It's true, baby," he says softly as he trails his fingertips down my jaw and gently pushes upward so that I'm coaxed into meeting his gaze. "It's not the wine, I'm the luckiest man alive because in just a few short months, I'm going to be your husband."

"Months?" I ask putting on my best faux appalled expression. "I'm going to need a minimum of two years to plan the perfect society wedding for your parents and their crowd."

"What?" he chokes out as he stops our swaying to the music.

"These things take time." I nod seriously.

"Years?" he asks on a smile.

"Years," I confirm. Wes looks me in the eye and I can't help but throw my head back and laugh.

Wes rolls his bottom lip in between his teeth and bites down as he studies me. I want to squirm under his gaze, my laugh caught in my throat as he no longer looks at me to evaluate the truth of my bold statement—which is a lie—but he now watches me with a hunger in his bright amber eyes. There's a certain . . . *carnality* to the way that he's looking at me in the middle of a room full to the brim of our closest friends and family.

I can't help but wonder if it's suddenly a little warm in here and fight back the urge to fan myself. Wes sees my discomfort and an incredibly sexy smirk plays on his mouth.

"Wicked minx," he says as his eyes twinkle with mischief. "I don't believe you."

"Why wouldn't you believe me," I play coy, nodding my head with my eyes wide. "I'm very trust worthy. I'm a police officer."

Wes pulls me in tight to his chest, his arms tight bands around my body. I let out a yip as he swats my ass in front of everyone in the middle of the polished wood of the club's dance floor.

"I don't know about that," he growls. "I think you like to play games with me, Claire. But you underestimated just how much I like to play games too. I think you'll find that I rise to the challenge." And then he crashes his lips down on mine. Wes kisses me hot and hungry, and I can't help but open my mouth under his.

I lose myself in Wes and his kiss. The world falls away as we hold on to each other. This year has been hard. Hell, the last twenty-five years can't even be called hard—that's the understatement of the year—and after all of it was said and done, Wes and I finally found our way back to each other. I knew when he said he was done fucking around that he was done. But most of all, I know that he loves me above all else, Wes was willing to fight me, and everyone else, until we made it here to this place that we are in right now.

Right now, it's just us, Wes and me. We walked through fire to get here and we made it.

As Wes mouth moves over mine there is a roaring in my ears. He's always had a strong pull over me but even this is too much. Or at least I think it is until Wes pulls back and smiles against my mouth. The roaring is still there. I feel my face heat when I realize that the noise is actually a room full of wine infused former Navy SEALs cheering and stomping their feet at the show that Wes and I were so happy to give them.

"*Hooyah!*" goes up all around the room.

I chance a look across the room at Wes's parents—who do not look happy—before Wes distracts me and the thought slips from my mind.

"Who invited this band of rebels, ruffians, and miscreants?" he asks me with a twinkle in his eye. I can't help but smile at him.

"You did, silly. I have it on good authority that the SEALs came with you," I inform my better half with wide eyes.

"So they did, good lady. So, they did," he says as he bows over my hand like an old-fashioned gentleman. I can't help but throw my head back and laugh.

"'Good lady'?" I question.

"Okay, that didn't work." He laughs as he twirls me around the room.

"Not so much."

"But it was worth a try." He shrugs his shoulder. "For you I would try anything." And I know that what he says is true. I duck my head in an uncharacteristic show of shyness as my face heats again and I let Wes tow and twirl me around the room.

"You know, I thought a bunch of cops were bad but . . ."

"Us SEALs put the term 'bad' to good use, baby." He shoots me a lascivious wink.

The music changes to something soft, slow, and decidedly more sensual. Wes pulls me in close and we sway for a little while. My body heating with each soft brush of his body against mine. Wes stops our movement but doesn't let go of me.

"So, what do you say, gorgeous? You wanna get out of here?"

And I answer him the only way I can. Ignoring the room full of people, the music, and the wine. The world around us disappears once more when I look into his beautiful whiskey eyes and give him the truth.

"Yes."

chapter 2

go all the way

Six weeks earlier . . .

"**W**ELL," MRS. O'CONNELL SAYS just a hair shorter than necessary. Her tone definitely doesn't say *I'm so happy to be here with my favorite son and his lovely girlfriend.* "Are you going to tell us why we all needed to be here?"

Here being *The Farmer's Market,* the best brunch place this side of the Hudson.

"Yes," my mom says with a twinkle in her eyes. She knows what's up. "Tell us what was so important." She winks.

Wes turns to me and smiles that panty melting smile, the one that always gets to me. The one that when I was a little girl always told me that everything was going to be alright. In his way—the way of us, Wes and Claire—he's telling me that everything will be okay. And it will . . . in the end.

I only hope there's minimal bloodshed. That's a bitch to get out in the wash.

Wes turns back to address the occupants of the massive table in the back of the restaurant that includes: my parents, Wes's parents, Lee, Emma, Anna, and my grandparents. "I asked Claire to marry me."

"*You what?*" both his parents shriek at the exact same time. I can't help but wonder if they rehearsed their reaction.

I look across the table to Emma and Anna. Anna had the grace to wince. Emma rolled her eyes before pretending to scratch her eyebrow in their direction with her middle finger. Liam, I notice, is biting his lip to keep from laughing as he watches Emma's less than patient display.

"I said, I asked Claire to marry me," he repeats as if they didn't hear him in the first place all while squeezing my thigh under the table. I wonder if he's afraid I'm going to run away. Well, I figure if I've come this far, I might as well go all the way.

"And she said . . ." Mrs. O'Connell hedges. What the hell does she think I said? Clearly, we brought everyone out to brunch to tell them that I said no. I turned him down so we're politely telling our families that we're going our separate ways like those celebrities who *consciously uncouple*. I snort as I crack the joke in my head and realize everyone is looking at me waiting for my answer. Whoops.

"Oh," I mumble a little embarrassed to be caught in front of the class not paying attention. "I guess I said yes."

"You guess, dear?" Wes's mom presses.

"No, I said yes. Wes and I are getting married," I tell her. My smile faltering to an awkward grimace.

"Are you sure that's wise, son?" Judge O'Connell asks. Even though I knew it was coming, I won't pretend that didn't sting. Although, I always knew Wes's parents did not approve of me. They were always honest about that one.

"Yes," Wes says calmly. "I do."

"I love hearing you say those words about my baby girl, son," my mom says to Wes with happy tears in her eyes.

"Welcome to the family, asshole." Lee laughs.

"Thanks, brother," he says tossing a roll at Lee.

"No, your father is right, Wesley," Mrs. O'Connell weighs in again. "We need to talk about this."

"No, we don't," Wes says, his voice low like a wolf's growl.

"Now, there's no need to get your back up. No one is saying you can't continue your relationship with Claire . . . privately," Mrs. O'Connell condescends.

"Don't," he bites out.

"Think about your father's political career." Mrs. O'Connell continues.

"No, I'm going to think about Claire and I and any children we might have."

"Children!" his father booms. "That's ridiculous. She will make a terrible mother."

"Thank you for your vote of confidence," I snap under my breath. I'm barely able to hold back my epic eye roll.

"You need to marry someone your own age who will add to this political family," Judge O'Connell orders.

"No, I don't. I will not be trotted out on your political campaigns anymore and neither will my wife."

"Of course, I will. I will do anything I damn well please and don't you forget it," Judge O'Connell seethes. This is a side of him I've never seen before. "Fuck her in private if you have to but for God sakes, don't throw both of our careers away over a piece of ass. Call me when you find a real wife who can benefit us all," he says before tossing his napkin on the table and pushing his seat back to stand.

"Don't bother contacting me," Wes says his voice low enough that only our table can hear. "I care about Claire and I always have. If you try and make me choose between her and you, I promise you won't like the consequences."

"Wesley—" his mother pleads.

"I mean it," he responds, his voice is low and calm, but also firm and unyielding.

His dad shakes his head before looking disappointed and then storms out of the restaurant. His mother pauses at our table to plead her case one more time but it falls on deaf ears.

"Look what you've done, Wesley. I hope you're happy," Mrs. O'Connell dresses down her grown son in front of a table full of people.

"I am. I only wish you could be happy for me."

"Mark my words, she'll ruin us all," my future mother-in-law tries one last time before giving up—for now—and following her husband's footsteps.

"Oh look!" my Nana shouts clapping her hands, she draws all of our attention. "Champagne! I love champagne!"

"Don't let those stuffed shirts bother you, baby

doll," my dad whispers in my ear from my other side. "Wes always fit in better with us than with them and it always rankled them a bit. They'll come around."

"That's what I'm afraid of, dad."

"Oh shit—I mean shoot—we need to book the church ASAP before some other Joe Schmo books it for their kid," my mom shouts as the thought obviously jumps into her head. "Do you kiddos have a date in mind?"

"Mom—" I start before she and my Grandma cut me off again.

"Goodness! There's just so much to do!"

"I don't know if we're going to get married in a church . . ." I add quietly.

"Of course, you'll get married in the church!" my grandma laughs as if I'm joking. I would correct her but truthfully, we're all a little afraid of her.

"See," my dad whispers in my ear. I can hear the laughter in his voice and I'm sorely tempted to stomp on his foot under the table. "There's nothing to worry about."

All around the table my mom and grandma, not to mention Emma and Anna, are planning our wedding. I can't help but sit back feeling a little shell shocked. I hear my dad finally lose his battle with the chuckle that's clearly been choking him to make its way out when I say to him, unable to break my gaze away from my life spinning wildly out of control, "I'm not so sure I agree with you, Dad."

He throws his head back and his soft chuckle gives way to a full booming laugh. I'm so glad he finds all of this so funny. Just wait until he gets the bill.

chapter 3

get there

Present day . . .

"SO, WHAT DO YOU say gorgeous? You wanna get out of here?" Wes smiles at me as the music changes again but I know that we won't segue into another dance at our engagement party. I place my hand in his outstretched one and answer him from my heart.

"Yes."

Wes leans in and kisses me hard and fast before walking me through the room, the skirt of my pretty black cocktail dress swishing around my thighs. As we make our way to the door, someone shouts, "Looks like this party just became a private one."

We push through the side door of the country club with a quiet clank as it shuts behind us. Wes and I, hand in hand, turn our heads to look at each other and laugh.

"That's my favorite sound," he whispers into the night.

"What?" I ask feeling a little confused and a lot of expensive wine.

"When you laugh."

"Wes—" I start but I'm cut off by his shrill whistle as he hails a cab to take us home.

"Let's go home," he says softly as he pulls the yellow door open for me and I bunch up my skirt to slide all the way across the cracked vinyl seat to make room for the only guy to ever hold my heart. He slides in beside me and pulls the door closed.

"827 Adolphia, and step on it," he says to the driver.

"If my wife looked like her, I'd be in a hurry too," he mumbles before pulling out into traffic. I smile at my lap while pulling my skirt flat nervously and my cheeks heat.

Wes leans into me and slides his nose down the skin behind my ear, whispering, "I love you."

"And I love you."

Through break neck twists and turns and a couple very yellow lights, Wes holds me tight in his arms. He skates his hands over all very appropriate places. But still, when we finally pull up to the front of his house in the suburb we grew up in, I'm still a little drunk and more than a little on fire.

Wes tosses some bills and a heavy tip to the driver before flinging open the door and pulling me out with him. He slams the door to the tune of the cabbie's laughter ringing in my ears and as I look at Wes, I can't help but let the smile grow wider across my face.

There is a twinkle in his eyes that I know now, after all that we have been through, is so much more than wine and lust. This is a lifetime of love. This is everything.

I have to practically run to keep up with Wes as his

long, muscular legs eat up the ground of the walkway to the front of his—soon to be our—house. He stops in front of the door and punches in the code on the dead bolt before swinging the heavy piece of wood and steel open and pulling us through.

Wes has gone a little crazy with home security ever since my near miss a few months ago.

But I don't have time to think of that now as the door slams closed and the lock tumbles over. Wes leans back against the door and slides his whiskey gaze over my body as I stand in the entryway. The laugh that threatens to burst free from me dies on my lips as my body heats like a fever rolling over my skin. I bite down on my bottom lip to quell the shudder that rolls through my body but there's no stopping it.

"You're so damn beautiful," Wes says, his voice rough.

"Wes—" I start but I barely get the words out. Wes stalks towards me with sure, even steps. When he reaches me, he pulls my body to his, crashing his lips down on mine.

"I love you, Claire," he whispers against my mouth. He tangles his fingers in my long hair. "So fucking much."

"And I love you." My words light him up from the inside out. His tongue swipes into my mouth and he groans at the taste.

"You're mine, Claire," Wes rumbles as he lifts me up so that his lips don't have to leave mine as he stalks down the hallway and up the stairs toward the master bedroom. I wrap my legs around his waist and we both groan as his hard length comes in contact with my center.

"Always."

"Damn-fucking-right," he growls as he slides my body down his, lowering my feet to the floor. "Turn around."

I do as he says, slowly turning around so that my back is to his front. I hear his rumble of approval and I let my eyelids drift lower as a happy glow settles over me. Wes uses his free hand to brush the heavy length of my hair over my shoulder to hang over my right breast.

I hold my breath as his unhurried hands lower the zipper on my little black dress. When the sides of the dark fabric slip apart, Wes slides his hands underneath the edges, his rough palms electrifying the skin of my back and shoulders as he guides my dress off my body, letting it pool around my heels on the floor.

I release a heavy breath just before he lets a fin-gertip trail down my spine, stopping at the clasp of my black lace bra, unhooking it in the process. It floats to the floor, joining my dress. We reaches around me and holds a heavy breast in each hand. His thumbs graze my nipples ever so slightly and I arch against his hard body behind me. Wes lowers his lips to my shoulder placing the softest of kisses there before straightening and ordering me in a rough voice, "Take off your pant-ies."

Keeping my legs straight, I hook my fingers into the black lace of my panties and bending at the waist lower them to the floor. As I do, my uncovered flesh slides against Wes's hard cock behind the wool and zipper of his slacks. My breath catches in my throat when I feel his heat and strength exactly where I need him. There's something to be said about being naked, vulnerable, and bent over in front of a fully clothed man. I give this to Wes freely, not because he demands it, but because he deserves it.

"Go lay down on the bed," he rumbles after I stand back up, kicking my discarded clothing aside and stepping free from the bulk of it.

Wearing nothing but my tall, strappy heels, I make my way over to the big bed and pull the bedding back before lowering myself down to the cool sheets. I turn to my back, propping myself up against the mountain of pillows.

Wes stands there fully clothed, radiating suppressed energy. Slowly, oh so slowly, he pops open the buttons on his collared shirt before parting the soft material and slowly sliding it down his body. The buckle of his belt clanks as he pulls it free from his slacks, letting it drop to the floor before toeing out of his shoes and pulling his socks from his feet. And I lay there in rapt attention as each piece of skin is uncovered.

I hold my breath as he reaches for the clasp on his slacks. I breathe again when he lowers the zipper and pushes his pants and underwear wear down his strong legs as one. His hard length springs free and I watch—fascinated as he grips it in his fist. He lets his head tip back on his shoulders

"Spread your legs," he rumbles as he slides his fist up and down his length. "Show me what's mine because this is all yours, baby."

Wes watches me through narrowed lids as I let my knees drop to the sides. My body burns from the inside out as I watch him watch me put myself on display for him. Only for him. My body burns hot from the wine and from Wes. He has always had this effect on me.

Slowly Wes stalks towards me before lowering himself to sit on the edge of the bed beside me. I lay perfectly still, holding my breath, waiting to see what his first move will be. Tonight, Wes will lead. Luckily for me, I don't have to wait long.

Wes watches the movements of his hand as he caresses my cheek with the back of his fingers before placing his palm flat between my breasts. He leans down and softly places his mouth on mine, soft and sweet to start before sliding his tongue into my mouth and taking it deeper. There is no hurry to his movements or frantic pace. To Wes, it seems as if he has all the time in the world, and we're getting married so he does, but I'm a little drunk and I want more. I want so much more.

I press my body to his as I nip at his bottom lip before soothing the hurt with my tongue. Wes smiles against my mouth and I know that he can see right through me. But then again, he's known me since forever.

"I want slow," he rumbles against my mouth.

"Uh-unh," I mumble as I wrap a leg around his hips trying to entice him to my way of thinking.

"But slow can be so . . . *rewarding*," he says as he circles my nipple with his fingertips before finally scraping his nail over the tip making me arch into him.

"I want fast while the champagne bubbles are still in my head," I say as I dig a heel into the mattress and roll taking Wes with me. We land with him on his back, diagonally across the middle of the bed and me gracelessly sprawled across his body. He grips my hips tight in his hands.

"Is this what you had in mind?" he asks as he smiles up at me.

"Yes." I smile triumphantly as I wiggle my hips to straddle Wes as he lies beneath me.

I lean forward to kiss him. I open my mouth to him, letting him control the kiss. I lose my head as I rock my body against his. When I break my mouth away to catch my breath, I push back, impaling myself on his hard length. We both let out a groan as we hold eat other tight, adjusting to the way that we fit together.

I smooth my palms over Wes's chest and scrape my nails down his abs before slowly rising up and then sliding back down his cock. He lets a hiss out between his teeth as I rise up on my knees and slowly slide back down again and again.

I brace myself on my hands, my palms pressing against Wes's tight abs as I slide up and down his length, faster and faster. There is a heat that spreads out over my body as I get closer and closer. I drop my head back letting my hair brush over his strong thighs. Wes arches his back to meet me.

He pushes his hands to glide up my sides from my hips before gripping one of my breasts in each hand. I place my own over his, encouraging him to squeeze me tighter, to pinch and pull my nipples as I ride him.

I bow backwards and feel the muscles of his legs tense behind me. My movements become more frantic as I try and get closer and closer before bending back forward and bracing myself against his chest again.

"Get there, baby," Wes says through gritted teeth.

"I-I'm trying," I cry out in almost a whine, but I can't care. I'm so close and yet . . . not. I keep pushing harder and harder but I'm not getting any closer to the edge and it's making me panicky.

"You gotta get there, baby," he growls as his hips rise up to meet me as I sink back down over him.

"I can't!" I cry out.

Before I know it, Wes is gripping me by the hips and pulling me up and up and up off his cock. He lifts me up and over, so that my upper body is hanging off the side of the bed, my fingertips barely brushing the carpet, and my most secret places right over his face.

Wes pulls me down to meet his mouth and presses his tongue over my clit hard and fast, not letting up for even a moment. I grip the edge of the comforter in my left-hand and the nails of my right-hand rake over the carpet. Panting, I'm not sure if I'm trying to get away from his sexual onslaught or if I'm trying to get even closer. I roll my hips and receive a masculine groan and a nip to my clit for my reward, sending me spiraling out of control as I come.

Wes knifes upward, taking me with him in one fluid move. I land on my back with Wes moving over me, sliding in deep. He hooks my left leg over his right arm lifting it higher, taking him deeper, while I wrap my right leg around his hip as he plunges hard and deep.

Before I know it, my body is heating up again. I rake my nails down Wes's back and he rolls his hips causing me to clench tight around him. I'm building again.

"Yes," he growls as he powers into my heat over and over again. "Give it to me. Again."

I'm helpless to stop it so I do, and Wes follows me over the edge, roaring out my name as he does. He tucks his face into the crook of my neck as our breathing slows and he lowers my leg.

"You're right," he rumbles in my ear after a minute or two of silence. "Fast was fun."

"I told you so," I purr as I stretch like a cat underneath him.

"We'll do slow next," he tells me seriously.

"Okay," I whisper and then we do just that, we go slow before drifting off to sleep in each other's arms with the world at our fingertips . . . or so it had seemed at the time. If only we had known we were on the cusp of losing everything, we might have played things a little differently.

chapter 4

light in the dark

IT'S DARK. SO, SO dark. And scary

At night my mommy leaves a nightlight on for me and my favorite piggy stuffed animal that I've had for ages to help me sleep. I hate the dark. Monsters only lurk in the dark. I want my mommy but I can't cry. If I cry, the bad man will come and he will hurt me again. He always hurts me. Even though I don't want him to, I know, he always comes, but this time I will be ready.

I was digging in the closet when I knew that he was asleep. I found a pile of old junk. He must have been too lazy to clean out the closet that has been my prison for I don't know how long. But his laziness is my win. In the corner under the pile of old stuff, I found a baseball and then a glove, and in the very bottom of the pile, I found an old metal bat. Just like the kind Liam and Wes used when they were my age.

Sometimes it pays to be the little sister. My whole life I've been following Wes and Liam around hoping that they would play with me. I even told Wes that one day he would marry me. He just laughed and said, "I'm not so sure about that, squirt." That's what he calls me. Squirt.

So, all the times I followed them around when they played ball or walked in the woods finally is going to pay off even if Wes never wants to marry me because I learned how to swing a baseball bat watching them. I learned to run through the woods following them. I am going to run away from the bad man because of all that I watched them do.

So, I wait. And I wait and I wait and I wait. I almost fall asleep. Almost. I feel my eyelids getting heavy but then I hear footsteps and I know that he's coming. He always comes.

So, I sit quietly and try not to make any noise. I hurry to my feet and grab my bat. I crouch in the corner with the bat over my shoulder just like Liam showed me how to do. When I hear the lock that he keeps on the closet door open I know that it's time.

My hands sweat and I feel shaky all over.

"Wake up, Claire, it's time," he says as he pulls open the closet door. "What are you doing?" He asks when he sees me but I don't answer. I swing the bat as hard as I can, hitting him in his big belly.

When the bad man falls forward, I swing one more time, hitting the side of his head just like Liam and Wes taught me to hit a baseball when I finally got them to include me. And then I run.

I run out of the closet while the bad man screams my name. I run out of the ugly house that smells funny and then I run out into the woods.

I run and I run and I run. But I know he's going

to catch me. A mean hand grabs me by my arm from behind and I scream . . .

I gasp, feeling the band tighten around my chest as the nightmare leaves me in its wake. Fuck, it's still happening. A small part of me had hoped that with my life finally becoming normal that the dreams would go away. But you know what they say about hope being a fickle bitch and all that . . .

My body is covered in a sheen of sweat, my head is pounding with the drums of the old Salvation Army band, and my stomach is roiling. I jump up and run to the bathroom, dropping down to my knees just in time to lose my very expensive celebratory dinner and champagne.

My body stiffens when I feel a hand brush my hair back from my face.

"Too much champagne?" he asks with a note of humor in his voice. The miserable bastard would just love for me to be hung over.

"Yeah," I whisper.

"Claire?" he asks. I hate the worry in his voice. I hate that I put it there. I thought I had escaped—that I was *finally* free—but I'm not free, I'll never be free. I've brought Wes straight into hell with me and I hate that most of all.

"Just let it go, Wes." My voice is rough in desperation, for him to leave it alone, to leave me to my own devices, I don't know which.

"No," he grounds out his voice firm. I hang my head unwilling to look at him yet. I can't stand that this is how he sees me, at my lowest, covered in sweat with the scent of vomit in the air.

"Wes—" I begin to plead but he stops me before I can even get the words out.

"No!" he shouts. "No, I won't let it go and no, I won't go away. I want in there, Claire. You have to let me in, baby." He's pleading, and I can't stand the desperation in his voice or the knowledge that I am solely responsible for it.

"It's too dark, Wes," I whisper. "I can't drag you further into hell with me."

Wes drops down onto his knees behind me, wrapping his arms around me as if he can block the world from seeping on to my shoulders. In this moment, Wes is my shield, my protector, my big, bad warrior and I know in my heart that with him I can do anything, be anything, but without him, I don't even want to try.

"I've already been to hell, honey," he says softly, his chin resting on my shoulder, reminding me that he has been to hell and knows its demons on a first name basis. "Let me walk in there with you. Let me be your light in the dark."

"It's not that easy."

"But what if it is?" He asks softly. "What if together we can beat it back?"

"I just don't know," I say softly, my voice harsh. "I'm so scared."

"I know, baby." His arms grip tighter around me, easing the invisible band around my chest. "Let me be your light."

"You already are."

And in this moment, I realize the veracity of my words. The power they hold rings true for both of us. No longer have I craved the bite of my own bullet and while I struggle with the nightmares, the trauma that still lives inside me, twisting me up, I no longer feel alone, because I'm not. Maybe, just maybe, we can beat back the darkness, together. Wes is right, it's time to let him in. If we're really lucky, I won't drag him into hell with me, but he might just be able to help me pull myself out once and for all.

"Then let's go back to bed," he whispers.

"Okay."

chapter 5

easy

RUNNING. I'M RUNNING AS *fast as I can.*

The tree branches sting my face as the slap at me and grab at me as I run past. The briars cut into my feet but I can't stop. I can never stop.

I trip over a tree root but don't fall. I have to keep running, running, running, I can't let the bad man get to me. I can never let him get to me.

I'm running as fast as my little feet will take me through the woods behind my parents' house. I have to get away from the bad man. If he catches me now, I'll never get away. I have to be free.

Run! I have to run faster.

I see the blue gray light as it spills through the trees. Mommy always told me this was her favorite part of the day—looking at the sun as it comes up in the morning. I ran away late in the night when the bad man was sleeping. It was my only chance. After he broke the lock on the closet door I knew that I had a chance to get out.

Free.

I'm free. Those are the words in my head as the trees break and I see Wes standing at the edge of the backyard. I'm free. I'm finally free. Wes looks up and he sees me.

"I've got her!" he shouts to someone.

My heart is beating so hard in my chest and it hurts to breathe. I'm so tired but I have to keep running. I see Wes, his face, and I know that he'll protect me. Wes always protects me. He will keep me safe. He will keep me free.

I push my feet just a little harder, I run just a little faster. I'm almost there. My feet are covered in blood and dirt, all of me is really. Wes is running towards me. No, Wes! The bad man is coming! I want to shout but when I open my mouth, no words come out.

Wes reaches for me, his arms out ready to grab me. This is good. I'm so tired. I just need to close my eyes for a second. I blink a few times to wake up again. Rest, I just need a little rest. Mommy will be happy, she's always trying to get me to nap.

"I've got you!" he says to me. "I've got you."

"Don't let me go," I say.

"Never! I'll never let you go," Wes declares in his strong voice and I know that he is telling me the truth. Wes is so strong and so brave. Mama says that he's going to go to the Navy with Lee and they only take the very bravest there is. So, I know that I'm safe here with him. I'm finally safe.

"I've got you," Wes rumbles from behind me. His

strong arms close around me.

"Don't let me go," I plead as I cling to him. "Don't ever let me go."

"Never, baby," he says squeezing me tighter. "How many times do I have to tell you. I'll never let you go."

"Good."

"Just be free and easy," he rumbles softly next to my ear and I feel the muscles in my body release their tension one by one, knowing that Wes is on duty and he's watching my back I drift back to sleep. This time it's a totally dreamless—*peaceful*—sleep.

Beep . . . beep . . . beep . . .

I groan as Wes reaches for his phone to silence his morning alarm. Saying it was a long night last night is the understatement of the century. We shouldn't have to wake up early the day after our engagement party. Come to think of it, we don't have to.

I scowl at Wes who is smiling bright. There is a wickedness twinkling in his eyes that I don't quite trust.

"What's that face all about, Mister?" I ask as I swirl my finger around in the air roughly circling Wes's face. The look in his eyes softens and his breath catches in the back of his throat before narrowing his eyes.

"Don't be cute," Wes reprimands me playfully. "I don't have time to properly fuck you."

"Who's being cute?" I ask seriously wondering. No one has ever accused me of being cute before and for

sure not before I've had a cup of coffee in the morning.

"Shit," he groans before tackling me to the bed. "Now I have to fuck you."

"Wes!" I screech as I land flat on my back with Wes looming over me, his hard length rubbing against my pussy creating a delicious friction under my panties.

"Don't worry," he says against my mouth. "I'll be quick."

"When are you ever 'quick'?" I laugh.

"Okay." He nods his head sitting back on his heels before sliding my panties down my legs. "I won't be quick, I'll be thorough. But we're going to have to get breakfast on the way."

"Deal," I say because Wes is circling his fingers around my entrance and there is no possible way that I can hold a decent conversation at this juncture in my life let alone a single thought in my head.

I grip the sheets in my hands and arch my back. I grind onto Wes's hand before he pulls it back shoving his shorts down and growling, "You're ready," before plunging inside me.

I wrap my arms and legs around him and cling tight as he thrusts deep and then slides back out over and over again electrifying me from the inside out. I rake my nails down his back and Wes tips his head back and groans.

Every slip and slide of his cock sends me closer and closer to the edge. I tip my hips to meet his every time needing that just a bit more to take me there. My body clenches around Wes and he knows how close I really am and picks up his pace.

He plunges in once, twice, and then three times be-

fore proclaiming, "You're there."

And I am.

"Wes—" I gasp out as he thrusts home one more time and then I am flying right over the edge.

"Claire," Wes growls as he plants himself deep within me and follows me over.

We lay together for what seems like ages and at the same time, never long enough, while our hearts slow and the sweat cools, clinging to each other. This has become one of my favorite moments with Wes. There is no pressure to be anything, to do anything, we simply just are. And we are together. There is a peace that I can only find inside of Wes's arms and I will do anything to keep it.

He slides the tip of his nose down the side of mine before kissing me quickly on the mouth. "It's never been like that with anyone before," he rumbles in his sex deep voice that I love so much.

"Wes." My breath catches in my throat.

"It's only every been you, Claire."

"Wes?" I ask.

"Yeah, baby?"

"Shut up," I say softly, smiling so he knows that I'm not being mean.

"I can't, baby. We've got places to go, people to see," he says before slipping free from my body and knifing out of the bed.

"And what would those places be?" I ask. "Who are these people?"

"Didn't I say before?" he asks playfully. I love this side of Wes that doesn't get to come out very often.

"No, dear, I'm pretty sure that you didn't."

"Oh," he says as if he's thinking seriously on the subject but we both know that he's not. "I guess I didn't," he says before scooping me up and throwing me over his shoulder, laughing as he goes.

"Wes!" I shout.

"I told you, we don't have time." Wes swats my ass hard and laughs as I growl. He swats me again. "We definitely don't have time for me to make you come in the shower so quit your wiggling. It does things to me."

"Would you quit doing that?" I snap.

"No." He shakes his head. "Probably not. You all fired up does things to me too."

"Seriously, Wes? Not everything can turn you on."

"Wanna take a bet?" he asks as he slowly lowers me down his body, his hard cock brushing against me as Wes lowers me to the ground. My feet touch the soft cotton of the bath mat.

"I stand corrected. Apparently, it doesn't take more than a stiff breeze."

"Not even that with you around," he says before grabbing me as he opens the shower door and hurdles us inside under the freezing cold water.

"Are you kidding me!" I screech.

"It should heat up soon." He shrugs.

"Soon?" I snap.

"Okay," he laughs. "I'll heat you up. I'll be quick this time. I promise." And then he does heat me up against the shower wall before soaping me up and tossing me out, drying me off with a towel as we go.

I need to talk to Anna about the dreams that seem to be coming on with more and more regularity. I don't understand what it all means. But for now, this morn-

ing, I have to find out what kind of surprise my guy has in store for me.

chapter 6

no fucking way

"YOU'VE GOT TO be fucking kidding me?"

"Now why would I kid about this?" Wes's laugh rumbles in his chest behind his words.

I clap my hands over my eyes. There is no possible way I saw what I think I saw. Wes loves me, he wouldn't try to kill me . . . at least, I'm pretty sure. Almost positive. I mean he went to all that trouble to save me a couple weeks ago. So, he wouldn't just off me now . . . I think.

"Babe, what are you doing?"

"I'm hoping that when I uncover my eyes there isn't a deathtrap standing in front of me," I answer him honestly before uncovering my eyes. "Nope, it's still there."

I cover them again as quickly as I can.

"I'm pretty sure your lady just offended me, O'Connell," someone says.

"She sure did, Palmer," Wes says with a smile in his voice. "And if you don't shut your mouth I'll tell her how you got that name."

"You mean Palmer isn't your last name?" I ask as everyone either snickers or groans.

"It's really a funny story . . ." Wes starts.

"Don't you fucking dare, or I'll push you out myself without a god damned shute," Palmer threatens. "I need at least a halfway decent chance with the cute bridesmaid."

"And which bridesmaid would that be?" I ask hoping to change the subject away from my impending doom.

"The cute little brunette. You know, the fancy one. I just want to dirty her up a bit."

"No, I want the hot blonde with the long legs and the smart mouth," someone else shouts. How many guys are here anyways?

"Good luck with that," I say. "You have my blessing. She could use a good dirtying."

"Thanks." He winks.

"Hey," I say after thinking better on just giving away my closest friend. "You're not a serial killer or anything? I've had my fill of those lately."

"Babe," Wes says with a little light censure in his tone.

"What?" I ask. "Too soon?"

"Yeah, honey. Too soon."

"Okay," I shrug.

"So are we going to do this or what, ladies?" Palmer asks.

"No," I say with my hands still firmly locked over my eyes. "I'm not doing anything."

"Claire," Wes says.

"No," I say shaking my head in the negative. Definitely not, he's asking too much.

"Would I ever do anything to hurt you?" he asks honestly.

"Well," I start ticking off his offenses on my fingers. "You took my virginity when I was eighteen and broke up with me the next morning causing me to never commit to another relationship again. Then there were the many times you tried to get my brother to fire me. Or there was the time you tried to steal my case from me. Actually, come to think of it, you did that a couple of times too. Then—"

"Alright!" he shouts. "We get it, I'm an asshole."

"Sounds like I should punch your nose again, brother," Lee says from somewhere near. Of course, I can't see him because my eyes are closed firmly in denial.

"Oh hey, Lee," I greet my brother casually.

"Hey there, Claire Bear."

"Come to rescue me from impending doom?" I ask but Wes's growl drones out all other conversation.

"You both should know damn well by now that I wouldn't do anything to physically hurt Claire or put her safety at risk." He sighs heavily like he usually does when he runs his hand through his hair. Usually after I have done or said something to drive him up a wall. "Now I have a dick so I'm going to fuck up from time to time."

"Sounds like you fuck up on the regular, O'Connell," someone chimes in.

"Here, here," I shout.

"Really?" Wes grumbles. I have to bite my lip to

keep from laughing out loud at poor Wes's outrage. He's really been a good sport about our ribbing him. I sigh heavily. I guess I'm going to have to let him try to kill me. I just won't make it very easy.

"Oh, very well," I say.

"You're going to do it?" Wes ask me.

"Yes," I answer. "I'm going to let you try and kill me."

"Hey!" Palmer shouts.

"Palmer really is a damned good pilot," Lee assures me. "If he says the bird is good to go, it is. Even if it looks like a steaming pile of shit that's about to fall out of the sky any minute."

"Thanks, man, that was really touching," Palmer says with mock sincerity.

"Anytime, buddy. Anytime." Lee laughs.

"Can we move along now, ladies," Wes taunts.

"Hey, Cupcake, what's the rush?" I begin to panic all over again.

"We only have the air space for so long today and we already took up some valuable time this morning because you didn't want me to rush," he whispers in my ear. Even though the others couldn't have heard his words my face still burns beet red.

"Oh, yeah. Right," I say softly. "Well, then, carry on."

"Thank you." He wraps his arms around me from behind. "But first you have to uncover your eyes. I promise you won't regret it."

"Fine," I say before slowly lowering my arms. Maybe it's not as bad as I originally thought it was. I slowly pry open my eyelids and . . . nope, it's still pretty fucking bad. "Okay. I'm ready."

Slowly he lowers himself to squatting behind me. Wes taps my legs to lift them. "Step into your harness, honey."

"Are you sure you're not having some weird bondage fantasies?" I snark.

"No, I have tons of fantasies and trussing you up like a Thanksgiving turkey is definitely one of them. This is just for fun."

"And a little kink isn't fun?" I ask. Wes turns and looks at me curiously.

"Trust me, baby, when we cut loose, fun isn't going to be any word near your mind in the moment. Maybe intense, or wild. You might beg me to let you come, but fun won't be part of it." At the end of his little monologue I'm breathing a little heavy and I'm trussed up like a turkey, just like Wes had said. Shit! How did that happen?

I look around and all of the other guys are in flight suits and jump gear. Even freaking Palmer!

"Hey! Why does the freaking pilot have a parachute?" I shout. "That's not right!"

"Your lady's concern for my welfare is endearing," Palmer says without looking up from his clipboard.

"It's Standard Operating Procedure, babe. Everyone on board needs one. Kind of a just in case thing." Wes shrugs.

"Just in case?" I shout, my voice is getting louder and louder.

"It's fine," he reassures me. "Everyone has one."

"I don't have one!" I shout.

"That's because I am your parachute. Nothing will

happen to you with me there." He sighs giving me huge puppy dog eyes. "Would you rather jump with Lee? We'd have to change some things around, but he can take you if you'd feel more comfortable."

He had to go and break my heart and make me feel like a grade A asshole all at once.

"No, Wes. I want you," I tell him honestly.

"Damn right, you do." He nods his approval.

"Okay." I clap. "Let's go die!"

"Not funny!" a bunch of the guys chime in.

"It was a little funny," I say as I follow them all onto the plane.

Palmer is standing at the opening between the interior of the plane and the cockpit, if you could call it that, with another man I vaguely remember meeting last night. Everyone has whispered about his belonging to an agency with initials and clandestine operations. The rest of us are sitting on rickety benches that line the sides of the plane with no seatbelts.

"There's no seatbelts," I harshly whisper. The other guys around me bite back smiles.

"Babe, we're not supposed to be in the plane when it lands," Wes explains.

"Oh, right." I look around wondering if anyone heard my blunder. I feel my face heat when I see a lot of smiling eyes looking at me.

"Alright, ladies. Listen up!" Palmer shouts. "Surfer will be your Jumpmaster today."

"Surfer?" I ask. "He looks so . . . *serious*."

"He is. He's also from San Diego. That's all it takes for a call sign," Wes explains to me. "Later I'll tell you all about how Palmer got his."

"There is no static line today as we have spare parts with us so free jumps it is," Palmer continues. "And no, you will not!"

"Hooyah!" They all shout in unison.

"I'll meet you all back at the hangar."

"Hooyah!"

"That's a little unnerving," I say as Palmer climbs into his seat and starts flipping switches to start the plane.

The plane bounces and rambles down the pothole lined runway before suddenly leaping into the air. It seems a little too ambitious of the little plane that couldn't. I hold my breath but before I know it we're climbing higher and higher until suddenly, Palmer shouts, "We've reached jump elevation."

"Oh fuck," I pant as I start to panic.

"Later," Wes say before placing a kiss on the corner of my mouth. "We'll do that later."

"Stand up!" Surfer shouts.

"Aye, aye!" they all shout in unison.

"Tandem, hook up," he says looking to Wes who starts clipping my harness to the front of his.

"I feel like there should be more here hooking us together like steel bars or a roll cage," I mumble.

"You'll be fine," Surfer says to me before winking. "Enjoy your walk in the clouds, Eyes." And then Wes pushes me out of a perfectly good airplane. Well, I guess it wasn't a *perfectly good* airplane, but still, it was an airplane and it was in the fucking sky.

"Open your eyes," he shouts to me and I do.

It's the most amazing thing I have ever seen. The sky is so bright, and the clouds feel so close that you could reach out and touch one. In fact, I do and Wes chuckles behind me. We soar over the tree tops and all too soon a field is coming into view.

And when Wes touches his boots to the ground in the most perfectly executed landing and keeps me from falling flat on my ass I think I'm glad I put my faith in him once again.

I guess I'm not going to die today after all.

"So, are you going to hook me up with the hot blonde bridesmaid or what?" I hear one of the guys ask Lee while we're all sitting around tables clustered together at some dive bar near the airport.

"No fucking way," Lee growls and I sigh to myself.

"You have to let them figure it out for themselves," Wes whispers into my ear and I realize my sigh wasn't to myself at all.

"I know." I don't know but I'm going along with Wes's sage advice . . . for now. No guarantees when it blows up in all our faces, but hey, what do I know?

"Sorry, man. I didn't know I was poaching."

"You're not." Lee sighs before looking directly at me for help, or to reassure me, I don't know what. "It's not poaching. She's just off limits."

"But the brunette isn't?" someone asks.

"No, she isn't," Lee answers. I can't help my flinch at his words and the sadness that crosses his eyes, so I look away as quickly as I can just like the coward that

I am.

"Sounds like there's a story there," someone says.

"With a woman there always is," Surfer says. "I think I need another beer." Then heads to the bar at the back of the building.

"Maybe some other time," Lee says.

"Yeah, some other time."

"I never figured you for a chicken?" Wes rumbles in my ear.

"Shut up," I snap, and Wes tosses his head back and laughs. The conversation quickly turns to what the guys have been up to over the years and how glad they are to be back together again. Surfer stays notably absent during the conversation.

Overall, it's been a great day.

Now, we're here in our bed, still snuggled together and it's the perfect ending to a beautiful day. Lying in bed with my head on Wes's chest, the blankets pulled up around me even though we're both still naked underneath them, skin to skin as the sweat cools down after he brought me back home after eating too many hot wings and drinking too much beer. All me not Wes. Then he made good on his promise to fuck me later and it was fabulous.

"Did you have a good day, baby?" Wes asks me, his voice soft and a little unsure.

"The very best of days," I whisper back. "Thank

you."

"Anytime, Claire. I would do anything to make you happy," he says as he twists a lock of my hair around his index finger studying the way the curl clings to his finger.

"I know that, Wes, and . . . thank you. But you have to know—"

"What is it, honey?" he asks with sincere interest both in his tone of voice and written on his face. I blink and take a deep breath before answering with the truth in my heart.

"That all of my best days have been with you."

"Mine too." Then we curled into each other as if we were born to do so and drifted off to sleep. If I dreamed at all, I was too tired to be bothered by it. I slept through the night and I did it in Wes's arms, right where I was meant to be, and I slept soundly . . . that is until I didn't sleep at all.

"Come out of the closet, baby."

"No," I whisper, tears hot on my face and snot stuffing up my nose.

Liam and Wes were right, I'm just a baby. A big kid wouldn't be crying in the dark corner of a closet hoping it'll all go away if you just wish hard enough. I bet Wes never cries. I know Lee doesn't.

"Come out now, Claire. Playtime is over."

"No," I cry louder. "Please don't make me."

"Now!" He growls as the closet door rattles. I gasp.

"Leave me alone!"

"Get out of the fucking closet, Claire!" He roars.

"Please no," I cry harder, my body shaking with each sob.

"When," he kicks his hard boots against the closet door and it shudders.

"Please."

"Are you," he kicks it again.

The doors are the kind with the slats that fold side-ways. We have them at home and mama says I always pinch my fingers in the accordion. Whatever that is.

"I just wanna go home," I whisper.

"Gonna," he kicks again.

"I just want my mommy," I sob. "Please. I just want my mommy."

"Fucking," the boards snaps and I scream.

"I just wanna go home, please," I beg.

"Learn!" he shouts as he kicks the broken boards out of the way. He leans down and grabs me by my up-per arms.

"Please," I wheeze but my words are cut short when he slaps my face hard. So hard I taste blood in my mouth and it's so yucky I feel sick. I'm going to throw up from the yucky taste. I try as hard as I can not to. I know that if I do, he'll punish me again. I don't want that. Anything but that.

"You are home, baby," he coos right before he slaps me again. I cry out again, falling to the floor with his last hit. It's so strong he knocks me down with it. "And I thought I told you to call me daddy," he says as

he lands a hard kick to my back.

"You're not my daddy, you'll never be my daddy," I whisper. "My daddy is a nice man. He would never hurt me. You'll never be my daddy," I say again but the bad man can't hear me, he already walked away. I have nowhere to go, but one thing is for sure, I have to escape.

I gasp and come awake all at once. I look over at Wes asleep in our bed with a happy look of contentment playing on his face and thankful for once that my personal nightmares didn't wake him.

I carefully slide out of bed and grab my phone off my nightstand before tip toeing my way out of our bedroom, carefully closing the door behind me. I tread softly through the hallway and down the stairs all the way through to the living room in the front of the house. As far away from the bedroom as possible because I do not want Wes to wake up and find me making this call in the middle of the night.

And it is a call I have to make, but one I am not sure that he would understand the necessity of.

I slide my finger across the cool glass surface to unlock my phone and dial the number that I know I can always call.

"Hello?" she answers in her sleepy voice.

"Hey, it's me," I say.

"Claire, is everything alright?" she asks.

"Yes," I start. "No. I don't know." I sigh.

"You had another nightmare," she says not asking a question. She doesn't need to. With me, Anna just knows.

"Yes."

"Do you want to tell me about it?" she asks me.

"No, but I need to," I tell her.

"Go on," she directs me to start.

"I keep dreaming about the events leading up to my escape."

"You're remembering more," she surmises.

"I don't know because the dreams are the same, but they are also always changing. It's the endings or the little details. I don't know what's up and what's down anymore and it's scaring me."

"The subconscious is a complex creature," she answers calmly. "It will take time for your brain to weed out fact from fiction, but I think that is exactly what you are doing. Let's not worry about the details right now as you're obviously trying to sift through those while you're sleeping. Those will come with time. I'm sure of it."

"Okay," I say.

"For now, let's work on some exercises to help you combat the panic when you do have a nightmare. What are you doing now when you have one?"

"I call you?" I ask, and she laughs.

"You are always welcome to call me, but what does Wes think about that?" After a pregnant pause she says, "Wes doesn't know you're calling me, does he?"

"No," I admit.

"Where are you hiding?" she asks.

"I'm not hiding, I'm in the living room," I blurt out and she laughs again. I sigh and then admit, "He wants me to let him in. To share my dreams and nightmares with him."

"And what did you say?" she asks me.

"I told him that I can't blindly lead him into hell with me."

"I can understand your feeling that way," she says. "I do, but I think Wes is a pretty tough guy. If he didn't want to be there or thought that he couldn't handle it, he wouldn't be there in the first place."

"Yeah," I agree. "That's pretty much what he said."

"What did he say exactly?" she asks.

"That he wants me to let him be my light in the dark."

"Well there you go," she says softly.

"Yeah," I agree.

"You think you can go back to sleep now?" she asks.

"Yeah," I answer. "I do."

"Okay then," she says softly. "I'll call you tomorrow and check in."

"Sounds good, Anna, and thanks."

"For what?" she asks.

"For everything."

"Anytime, honey," she says honestly. "Get some sleep."

"You too." She hangs up and I pad back up the stairs, down the hall and, quietly click open the door to our room before climbing back in bed with Wes. In his sleep he pulls me back into his arms and I let myself go, drifting off into sleep.

chapter 7

someone else's ass

I'M WARM AND SAFE *cocooned in the fluffy comforter on Wes's bed—our bed. The room is gently bright in a soft light that I can see through my eyelids.*

This is the most fabulous dream. It's about time I had a good dream, one where I am wrapped up in all the goodness that is Wes. The place where I am finally safe and whole again.

He places soft kisses at the joint between my neck and shoulder, moving his mouth slowly over one of my most sensitive places. It always drives me a little wild and heats me up when Wes does it. Speaking of heat, I'm warm, warmer than I had originally thought but too hot to be under this blanket.

I'm on fire but not in a bad way.

"Come back to me, baby," Wes rumbles against my shoulder. His morning bristles scrape my skin. "It's time to wake up." I growl in response.

Wake up? Why would I want to wake up? This is an amazing dream. He's lighting me up from the inside out.

"Come back to me," he rasps next to my ear.

My eyes flutter open and I realize that it wasn't a dream and I'm not trapped under the blankets, I am wrapped up in the safety and warmth of Wes's arms—his heat and strength and weight. Wes is placing soft, open mouthed kisses on my neck and shoulder, but the heat might just be coming from the way that I am rocking my hips and sliding my center along his hard cock that I have trapped between my thighs. *Whoops.*

"Wes," I breathe.

He lowers his hands from my waist, sliding them down around my hips to press firmly against my belly as he tips his hips back and slides all the way in to the hilt. The way that he presses his hand against my belly makes me feel so full and achy. I clench around him.

"Wes," I gasp as he gently rocks our bodies, gliding in and out, in and out. His movements are slow and steady as he softly rocks his body into mine. This coupling isn't a hurried fuck but a tender coming together.

"Yeah, baby," he rumbles as his other arm wraps tightly around me holding me securely to him.

"Yes." I tip my head back, resting it on his shoulder as he slides his cock into the heat of my waiting pussy at a maddeningly slow pace but still I can't stop the climax that's building within me like a low wave cresting in the ocean.

"That's it, baby," Wes encourages as he rocks his body into mine again and again.

"Yes," I say for lack of anything else. He has my mind totally wiped of all thought.

"You're almost there." And I am. I so am.

"Yes," I pant in agreement.

Wes slides in and out once, twice, and I cling to his arms that hold me tight, desperate for something to ground me. He pumps his hips one more time and I arch back against him, screaming, "Wes!"

"Claire, Claire, Claire . . ." Wes chants my name over and over again until he finds his own bliss.

We lay there in silence, wrapped up in each other, the walls we had erected so many years ago are finally in taters all around. There is nothing left between Wes and I anymore and if we work hard enough at it, there never will be again.

My heart is finally cracked open wide in Wes's hands and I couldn't be happier.

Our quiet peace is interrupted by the *beep . . . beep . . . beep . . .* of Wes's alarm clock signaling that it's time to wake up and begin the day. When Wes reaches over to silence it, I still his arm placing my hand on him and touching my mouth softly to his.

"What was that for?" he asks.

"Because I love you is all."

"Goodnite!" my brother shouts from within his office as soon as I walk through the front door of the station and pass into the bullpen. "Get in here. Now!"

"You know, I have always wondered how he does that?" I hear Wes muse from beside me. He claimed this morning that there was something he wanted to see Lee about before heading to his own office for the day, so he had followed me into the station instead of continuing to his own office. "It's uncanny really."

"I'm pretty sure he has me bugged somewhere, I just haven't found it yet," I say as I turn the pockets of my jeans inside out. Wes notices my actions and laughs as he pushes open the door to Lee's office.

"Maybe it's lojack?" he says on a laugh.

I sigh. I wouldn't put it past my brother to have some kind of GPS tracker or RFID key somewhere on my body. I start to wonder if maybe I have an implant somewhere like a dog when we push open Lee's office door.

"What's up, Lee?" I ask.

"I got a missing person for you," he barks.

"Well, good morning to you too, asshole," I grumble under my breath.

"God dammit, Claire!" he shouts.

"Who is it?" I ask.

"Kerrigan Adams," Lee answers.

"Why does that names sound familiar?"

"Because she went to school with Lee and I," Wes tells me.

"Oh, right. I remember her! She had huge . . . *you know*." I hold my hands way out in front of me to explain the attributes that a teenage Lee had found most appealing. "Lee had the hots for her and she wouldn't give him the time of day."

"Would you cut me some slack? Today of all days?" Lee gripes.

"Uhh . . . sure." I'm not really sure at all what has Lee so spun up but I guess he'll tell me when he's ready. Until then we're all just along for the ride.

"What's going on, Lee?" Wes asks.

"Isn't it fucking obvious?" he snaps. "My life is a fucking wreck." So many f-bombs, my goodness. I really want to point that out, but it would probably just make it worse.

"You're right," I snark. "It must be so hard being the big, bad Police Captain who loves to lord his rank over his lowly detective sister."

"Really, Claire?" Lee raises one eyebrow.

"I'm pretty sure he's talking about Emma, honey," Wes stage whispers.

"Ohhh, right. How's that going for you?" I ask Lee.

"Not fucking great. Also, thanks for the sympathy. I'm so glad my broken heart brings you, sister dear, joy."

"Your heartache doesn't bring me joy," I sigh. "I just don't know how to sympathize with you because you're breaking the hearts of both of my friends. I kind of want to kick your ass for messing with them in the first place, Lee."

"I know, I know," he holds his hands up in mock surrender. "I was wrong to fuck and run the way that I was, and I never should have touched either Anna or Emma, but now? Now I can't go back. I'm in love with her, Claire."

"And Anna is in love with you," I say sadly.

"Yeah," he agrees dejectedly. "So, what do I do?"

"Nothing," I tell him. "You're fucked."

"What the hell, Claire!" Lee shouts.

"What?" I ask. "You made this bed and I don't have any answers other than stop messing with my friends and fucking lay in it. They both look like their puppies have been kicked lately and I fucking hate it."

"I don't know," he says before injecting some steel in his spine. "Now get the fuck out of my office."

"Not so fast," Wes says. "I have something I need to talk to you about."

"I'm pretty sure I don't want to hear about you banging my sister so . . ." Lee laughs when I pull face.

"Go chew someone else's ass, douche canoe. We didn't fuck up your life, you did that all on your own," I snap.

"You're right," he says. "I'm sorry. Go on."

"I wanted to ask you to be my best man," Wes says looking at little green at all the displays of emotion lately. Lee looks pretty choked up too as he rises from behind his desk and hurries around to wrap Wes in a big bear hug.

"I'd be honored, brother," he says clapping him on the back the way that men do. It's so weird, you know what women don't do? Beat on each other to show our affection.

"Awe, that's precious," I snicker.

"I'd watch it, baby sister," Lee warns. "I wouldn't want the guys in the bullpen to hear about how you screamed like a little girl during your jump yesterday."

"I did not!" I protest.

"You kind of did, babe." Wes laughs.

"Well, even if I did, you can't prove it," I snap.

"You're right it would be your word against mine . . ." Lee says baiting me.

"That's what I thought—" I start.

"If I didn't have a video," he finishes.

"What video?" I jump. He wouldn't? He couldn't possible have a video, could he?

"The one I took of the jump," Lee says triumphantly. "I was behind you with a GoPro." Well fuck me running.

"I hate you," I tell my brother.

"No, you don't. You love me."

"I think I have a missing person to look for," I say as I snatch up the folder from Lee's desk and storm out of his office with their raucous laughter chasing me on my heels. "Don't forget we have a family dinner at Mom and Dad's tonight, assholes. Attendance is fucking mandatory according to Gran," I toss over my shoulder on my way out.

chapter 8

gone

WHAT A SHIT SHOW those two are. Sometimes I wonder if I'm the third wheel in this scenario. *Oh God, what if I'm the Yoko in this equation?*

I shake off those negative thoughts and drop down into my rickety desk chair with its five out of six functioning wheels and drop the file down on top of my desk flipping it open as I go. Kerrigan Adams is thirty-eight years old and a graduate of George Washington High School, class of 1998, along with Wes and Lee just like they had said. She is unmarried and without children. According to her office she never showed for work Friday morning and they became concerned. They contacted her parents, Mike and Molly Adams, who called it in.

I scoop up my keys and head over to Mr. and Mrs. Adams's house. They live over in the old neighborhood not too far from where Wes and I live now—or I will as soon as I finish dragging my shit over from my apartment. Part of me wants to just leave it and buy new shit because packing sucks.

I jump in my department Tahoe, which stays at the station more and more lately as Wes likes to ride to work together. After being apart for twelve years, then my almost being killed a couple of times, Wes has become a little clingy. At least he stopped trying to get me to quit my job.

The drive to the Adams's home is a silent one. I don't often listen to music or podcasts or whatever while working because I like to be lost in my own thoughts. I like to take every moment to go over what I know about the case whenever I have a free moment. You never know when something might click into place and send you on the right path.

I pull over and park next to the curb across the street from the Adams's family home. I see the curtains flutter and am not surprised. I would be nervous too if my daughter was missing. No matter how old she might be.

I will probably be the kind of mom that hovers after everything I have seen as a police officer and because of my own experiences that still haunt me almost every night. The thought of having Wes's daughter crosses my mind and for the first time in my life, I am excited at the prospect of having a baby.

I pull my keys from the ignition and step down from my truck. I walk across the street and up the front walk with a purpose. I don't like to leave people waiting or feeling like I'm not taking their case seriously. The truth is, I take every case more seriously than I should and ever missing persons case comes home with me and snuggles in my bed, unwilling to let me go from its grip late at night. These cases haunt me as much as the mystery of my own does.

I am not surprised when the front door opens before I have a chance to ring the bell. A woman in her early sixties with graying dark hair stands before me worrying a tissue in her hands. Her eyes are red rimmed. She's dressed in navy blue slacks with a crease pressed down the front of the legs and a light blue, short-sleeved sweater.

"Mrs. Adams?" I ask. When she nods I continue. "I'm Detective Goodnite with the George Washington Township PD. I'm here about your daughter, Kerrigan. May I ask you a few questions?"

"Yes," she says sounds like she's trying to catch her breath. I hear the sniffle behind her voice. "Please come in."

"Thank you," I say politely before following her into a family room in the back of the house.

"May I get you some coffee or tea?" she asks me.

"No, thank you, ma'am," I decline.

She nods before shouting over her shoulder, "Mike, the police are here about Kerrigan!" She turns to me as she sits down across from me. "My husband will be right down. He'll want to be here, so we don't miss anything. He's just beside himself. He and Kerrigan are very close."

"I understand." I smile softly. "I'm sorry that you're going through this but we're going to do everything we can."

"Thank you," she whispers.

A large man in his sixties dressed in a pair of khakis and a short-sleeved button-down shirt lumbers into the room stopping by Mrs. Adams's side. "I'm Mike Adams," he tells me as he holds out his hand for me to shake. I stand and take his hand. "My Molly says you're with the police department."

"Yes, Sir. My name is Detective Claire Goodnight with the George Washington Township PD. I'm here to ask you a few questions about your daughter, Kerrigan." He visibly suffers hearing her name, shuddering before nodding his head.

"Yes, ma'am. We'll do anything to find our girl." And I can hear the veracity of his statement. The hard truth is that these sweet, loving people would do anything to bring their daughter home safely and chances are that's not going to happen. Hopefully, she's shacked up in Atlantic City with a secret lover.

"What can you tell me about Kerrigan?" I ask as I pull a small notebook and pen from my pocket.

"She's a good girl," her mother informs me. "She goes to church and works an honest job. She is home every Sunday night for dinner." I smile at her. I too spend a lot of time with my own family. We're not that different from the Adams.

"And where does she work?"

"She works for Smith and Redmond Financial as a tax accountant."

"She the best damned accountant they've ever had," her dad says obviously taking great pride in his only daughter.

"And about how long has she been working there?" I ask.

"Ever since she interned there in college. She was hired on right away," Mrs. Adams tells me. "Where could my baby have gone?" she sobs obviously losing her composure. "She's just . . . *gone.*"

"I don't know, Mrs. Adams, but I'm going to do my best to find out."

"Please do."

"Was she seeing anyone in particular?" I ask after giving them a moment to regain their composure.

"No," Mr. Adams answers. "She and her college boyfriend broke up about a year ago. They never married or had kids. And her high school boyfriend is a priest now." Ouch. That had to sting. Nothing like knowing that after you your boyfriend chose celibacy and God.

After spending some more time with the Adams, answering their questions to the best of my abilities and asking a few more of my own, I bid them farewell.

"I'll be in contact," I promise. "As soon as I can."

"Thank you," Mrs. Adams says before shutting the front door behind me.

I climb in my Tahoe and start the engine, wondering to myself, where could Kerrigan have gone? By all appearances, she's the perfect woman, but somehow, some way, she got lost and I need to find her.

My phone rings in the cup holder where I had placed it when I climbed in. I answer and hit the speaker button so that I can drive.

"Goodnite," I answer.

"Hey, chick-a-boo, feel like breaking for lunch?" Emma asks me. I look at the clock on the dash and see that it's about noon. By the time I get back to the part of town where the station is located it will be almost one.

"I can meet you in about forty minutes," I answer. "I was out on a call."

"Sounds good," she says. *"Meet Anna and I at Luca's Deli at a quarter till."*

"I'll be there," I tell her before ending the call. I head back to the station.

chapter 9

let go

"SO, WHAT'S KICKING, LADIES?" I ask as I plop into the booth after ordering a turkey and cheese sandwich and a lemonade.

"We were just commiserating, that's all," Emma sighs.

"Yeah, nothing you would be interested in." Anna winks at me. "Besides, what's new with you?"

"Well tonight is a mandatory family dinner at mom and dad's, all hands-on deck. Something about wedding prep." I shrug. "I don't know."

"I'm in," Anna says. "I've got a vested interest to not wear anything hideous or polyester."

"Me too," Emma adds. "And I've got nowhere to be."

"That's a recipe for disaster but I'll tell mom you guys are coming." I laugh. "And back to the original topic, I'm interested in everything you two do. What are we commiserating about?"

"Bad dates," The say simultaneously.

"Oh man, I've had some doozies. Buckle your seatbelts, girls." I laugh. "Did I ever tell you about the guy that talked non-stop about his iPhone. It was ridiculous. He had all these extras and a special backpack that connected to his Bluetooth! I couldn't take it. After we paid the check I left and ignored his calls for four days before he finally gave up calling."

"That's nothing!" Emma laughs. The last date I went on asked me if he could suck on my toes. Before the wine was even served!"

"Maybe you'd like it." I shrug.

"Maybe I want a decent, stand-up guy with a monster dick in his pants," Emma says with her usual candor. "One who isn't so free with sharing said monster."

"That is basically asking for the Chupacabra and Bigfoot to have a unicorn baby and name him squishy," Anna laments.

"Besides, Claire," Emma smiles at me to soften the blow. "Your opinion on this subject is now no longer valid."

"What?" I laugh. "My opinion is always valid. And right too."

"No way." Anna winks. "You got your happily ever after."

"Right?" Emma agrees. "That's the Holy Grail." I open my mouth to disagree with them to make them feel better, but I stop myself before the words can come it. It feels like if I lessen the importance of what Wes and I have, even to make my friends feel a little better, that it's a betrayal to Wes. I just can't do that.

We're treading into dangerous territory here, I want to dodge and evade as much as possible. If we tread onto Lee territory at least one of my friends, if not both will end up hurt and broken. My brother is a great guy and I love him with all my heart, but he's a grade A asshole with women and he always has been. I'm pretty sure I was up front about that with both of my friends and they both jumped on his magic stick hoping for the best.

"Holy shit!" I laugh. The kid delivering our baskets of sandwiches and chips looks a little shell shocked obviously having caught part of our conversation. He drops those baskets and beat feet out of there. "Feet? But is that as bad as the guy I hooked up with from the station and two days later he'd had a case of guilty conscience and told his girlfriend *in Maryland* about it. She kept messaging me on social media to tell me what a whore I was. But I didn't even know he had a girlfriend! If anyone was a whore, it was him and not me. At least he transferred to a Maryland department shortly after."

"I'm pretty sure he didn't make that choice on his own," Emma says vaguely.

"Oh, I know. Liam told him he should strongly consider moving closer to his girlfriend for his own personal safety. I hear they're married, have roughly seventy-five children, and he fucks anything that breathes." I shrug. "Not my problem and it never was. He was a one off."

"I never got how you could be so cavalier about relations," Anna chimes in.

"I never wanted to get attached. Men do it all the time, why should I have been any different just because I have boobs and a vagina?" Too late, I realized my mistake. There was no way I could back pedal and not look like an asshole so Emma and I just stay silent while we watch Anna's face crumple.

Why couldn't I have just kept my fucking mouth shut?

"I'm sorry," I say.

"It's so stupid," she says, wiping her eyes with her fingertips. "It was one night, I knew he was only ever going to give me one night, I had just hoped . . ."

"Anna—"

"Like I said, stupid."

"The fuck it is!" Emma thunders. "He is such an asshole."

"No, he's not and you know it. He's a great guy." Anna takes a deep breath before pressing on. "I just need to let go, and I know it. But it's so hard and I want him so bad. You know what they say?"

"What's that?" I ask.

"You can't always get what you want," Anna answers.

"Or maybe we want the things that are bad for us," I say softly to Anna but really, to both of them. I love my brother and shouldn't speak ill of him, but he is toxic for both of them and they can do so much better.

"Anna, he's a jerk really," Emma pleads. "You don't know what he's done—"

"I do," she says quietly. "And it's okay. I love him enough that I want him to be happy. I want you to be happy too."

"I am happy," Emma denies.

"Are you?" she asks in her quack voice. Man, I hate when she turns those questions on me. It feels pretty good to see her point them at someone else for a change. I know that if I could see my face I would see a gleefully smug smile on my face. It's a little evil of me and I'm pretty okay with that.

"I'm happier without him than I would ever be with him. If he was so great he wouldn't be doing this—*to either of us*. He would just ride off into the sunset with you and live happily ever after," Emma explains her and I have to say, her logic is pretty sound.

"Only in my dreams." Anna sighs. "I just wished that I was enough, you know?"

"You *are* enough," I tell her.

"If anything," Emma snaps. "He's not good enough for you."

Anna shoots Emma a watery smile. "It's sweet of you to say. And I do appreciate it, but we all know that it's true. Sometimes, I just don't feel like I belong, you know? With you guys and Wes and Lee. Everyone is this badass with a gun, not afraid to get down and dirty with crime and I'm just . . . *me*."

"What?" Now I'm shouting. "Of course, you belong!"

"I know, and I do, but I also don't. I'm not a tough police officer. I drive a Mercedes. I'm just . . . different from you guys."

"Don't let that dick make you feel like you don't fit in because you do," Emma practically shouts. I can hear the tension in her voice, the strain of this love triangle is really getting to her.

"It's okay, really," Anna says, her voice is small, and I hate it. "I'm different and I know it. Anyways, I should go."

"You don't have to," I say but I know we all have to get back on the clock soon. She shoots me a watery smile before standing up and clearing her basket on the way out the door.

"Emma—" I start.

"Don't say it." She doesn't want to hear the truth, the real problem with her predicament. If Lee was just fooling around with them it would be one thing, but feelings are involved in a perfect storm of disaster and heartbreak.

"He loves you," I finish quietly.

"I love her more and he's tearing her apart."

"And what about you?" I ask. "Is this tearing you apart too?"

"None of that matters, and . . . well . . . he's an asshole. Plus, you know what they say? You can't always get what you want," she says sadly before following Anna out the door.

chapter 10

harmless little crush

MY HEART IS HEAVY.

My concern for both of my closest friends and my only brother is growing not by leaps and bounds but by mountains and valleys. There is no way the three of them can come out of this twisted love triangle unscathed.

But I have a missing person to find—yet, another woman from Liam's sorted past—so I toss my trash in the receptacle and place my basket on top of it before heading out to my Tahoe. I need to head over to Smith and Redmond Financial to poke around a bit.

The accounting office is on this side of town, so it doesn't take too long to get there. It's a small brown building next to a pizzeria and behind an old school diner, one of the ones shaped like a gigantic tin Twinkie. My stomach growls. I could literally eat all day long. It's kind of a situation.

I pull into the small parking lot behind the building and park my car. Then walk through the small alleyway that lets out on the main street a couple of doors down from Smith and Redmond, dodging the cracks in the sidewalk as I go.

I pull open the glass front door and a little bell overhead tinkles. A young brunette with thick glasses smiles at me from a small desk.

"May I help you?" she asks me.

"Yes, I'm Detective Goodnite with the George Washington Township PD and I'd like to speak to the owner if I may," I answer with a gentle smile on my face as I point to my badge on my hip to keep her from panicking. You never know who will panic when they see the cops.

"Mr. Redmond is in," she says. "I'll just go get him really quick."

"Thank you." I smile politely at her.

I look up at the sounds of footsteps on cheap office carpet and see the brunette leading a slim man with salt and pepper hair towards me. I catch him giving me a carnal appraisal with a crooked grin on his face. Over a year ago, I would have given him a chance but that was before Wes stormed back into my life and turned it all upside down. What a difference a year makes.

"Mr. Redmond, I presume," I greet him holding out my hand to shake his.

"I am. What can I do for you officer?" I feel my smile turn a little brittle at his honest question. I do my best not to roll my eyes. I mean, it's not his fault that he's kind of a sexist asshole. I guess that's not a very fair judgment but why can't they just assume the chick with the badge is a detective?

"I'm Detective Goodnite with the George Washington Township PD. I'm here to ask you a few questions about Kerrigan Adams."

Concern flashes across his face raising my own value of him. "Is everything alright?"

"Miss Adams has been reported as missing."

"I had hoped that wasn't the case." He sighs looking a little world weary. "Please, step into my office. We'll have more privacy there.

I follow him down the hallway of gray, nondescript office cubicles to his own office with several short glass windows peering out over the sea of cubes and middle management. I can't help but think that there is no way in hell that I could ever work here. I would slowly wither and die if trapped in this colorless world of numbers and boredom.

"Please, have a seat." He gestures to the crappy, uncomfortable looking chairs in front of his desk. Instead of sitting behind his desk he lowers himself to the chair next to mine. The chair that is *very* close to mine. It's both a little awkward and inappropriate. Not wanting to show that he is making me uncomfortable or off balance I force myself to stay rooted in my seat, taking out my little notebook and pen.

"What can you tell me Kerrigan Adams?" I ask.

"She's a great employee. Smart, beautiful, the whole package."

"The police report states that you called her parents when she was a no show here?"

"Yes," he answers.

"Is that normal for her?" I ask.

"Not at all," he answers. "Kerrigan is very responsible. Dependable. She's a diligent worker."

"Is Kerrigan involved with anyone here in the office?" I ask. His brow creases in thought over my question. Interesting because it should be an easy one—yes or no.

"My partner, Ken Smith, has had feelings for her for a while, but Kerrigan is unaware of how he feels."

"Would Mr. Smith be likely to stalk or abduct Miss Adams?" I ask.

"Not at all," he says sounding surprised by my question. "He's harmless. And more than that, he's heartbroken that she's missing."

"Were his feelings for her more than a crush?" I ask needing to know.

"No."

"Would you consider him obsessed with her or the idea of being with her?"

"No. Not at all."

"Is he in the office today?" I ask him.

"No, his mother had a heart attack early yesterday evening. He's been at the hospital with her ever since," he says sadly.

"Did anyone else here have a history with Kerrigan?"

Mr. Redmond pauses, he's obviously trying to weigh his words. "She and I had a . . . dalliance about two years ago. It was a onetime thing and before I knew how Ken felt about her. We never saw each other in that way again," he answers. I appreciate his candor. There was a lot there I wouldn't want to share if I was in his shoes.

"Thank you."

"It was just a way to scratch an itch, you know?"

He shrugs looking a little concerned.

"Thank you for your candor."

"This might not be totally appropriate, but . . . are you seeing anyone?" he asks.

I opt not to inform him how inappropriate it is to ask me and simply just answer the later part of his question. "I am. I'll let you know if I have any more questions. Thank you for your time, Mr. Redmond."

I stand and see my way out, walking around the corner and back through the little alleyway wondering just where Kerrigan Adams has gone. By all accounts she lives a quiet life of accounting, church, and family dinners with her older parents.

I jump in my Tahoe and start the engine. I head back to the station thinking I need to look into Mr. Ken Smith. Maybe, just maybe, his infatuation is more than just a harmless little crush.

My phone rings. "Goodnite," I answer after hitting the speaker button.

"Hey, baby," Wes answers and I can hear the smile in his voice. "How's your day going?"

"Pretty good," I answer. "I have relatively no leads on a missing persons."

"Let me know if you need any help," he offers genuinely.

"Stay out of my case, Suit." I hit my turn signal and turn left on Main Street. The station isn't too far from here but it's rush hour traffic at its finest in New Jersey.

"It's a genuine offer, Claire," he says softly. I must have hurt his feelings with my less than smart quip. I need to remember that it wasn't too long ago that Wes and I were head to head over a case and it was fairly ugly. I need to get this conversation back on track and quick.

"I know, I know," I gripe. "How goes it in Fed-Landia?" I ask.

"Not too shabby." He laughs. "Hey, I'm calling because I was wondering about mandatory family dinner night?"

"You mean you're not calling just to hear the sounds of my glorious voice?" I ask with faux shock. "I'm hurt, Wesley, truly."

"Very funny, kid." I grumble at his long worn out reference to my being too young. He's joking but it still strikes a nerve.

"What do you want to know?" I sigh.

"Do you want to meet me at your parents' house or do you want me to pick you up at the station?"

"I'm heading back to the station now, come and get me, big guy. I feel like at this juncture we should present a united front." Wes laughs.

"Sure thing, honey." His throaty chuckle flows over the phone lines reminding me again how much I enjoy his company. "I'll see you in ten."

chapter 11

united front

EVERYTHING'S GOING TO BE FINE. There is nothing to worry about going to dinner at my parents' house and other lies I tell myself with a regular frequency. I love my family, I'm not a monster after all, but they can be a lot to handle on a good day. And today is not a good day.

I mean it is, but Wes and I have handed them an impending wedding on a silver platter. We might as well have given them a golden goose with its ass stuffed full of diamonds and tickets to every World Series, Stanley Cup, and Super Bowl combined for the next forty years.

To sum it up, I'm nervous. What the hell were we thinking? Wes and I should have just run off to Vegas—an idea which I'm growing more and more fond of by the second—without telling anyone and sending them a postcard later.

By the time I pull into the parking lot behind the station where I lock up my Tahoe at night when I don't take it home I have worked myself up into a frenzy. There's not enough anxiety medication and booze in the world to talk me down off this ledge.

I turn the key in the ignition while doing some deep breathing and I look over. Wes is leaning casually against his Fed car with a *Rebel Without a Cause* cool. His suit coat is off, probably somewhere in the backseat of his car along with his tie. The top three buttons of his crisp, white shirt are popped open exposing his golden throat. His eyes are hidden behind a pair of dark black wayfarers, but I know that he's had a lock on me before I ever pulled into this lot. The thought has me warming from the inside out and my toes curling in my favorite boots.

Is it getting hot in here? I mentally fan myself, step down from the Tahoe, and make my way toward Wes. Awkwardly, I tuck a stray lock of my dark hair behind my ear.

"Hey, baby, you wanna get out of here?" he asks like all of my teenage fantasies of him rolled up into one memorable moment.

"Yeah." I smile at him. I'm genuinely happy to see him. He is a bright spot in my days.

"Then let's go," he says rounding the hood of his car and opening the passenger door for me. I drop down into the seat and tuck my long legs in.

"Thanks."

"Anytime." He gently closes the door behind me before walking back around the car and climbing in the driver's seat.

The drive back to the old neighborhood is longer than usual with rush hour traffic but still no more than twenty or thirty minutes. I continue to worry the entire time. As Wes drives down the turnpike with his eyes never leaving the road, I can tell that he sees all of my secrets. He knows I'm getting more and more nervous. Wes places his heavy palm on my thigh without saying a word. He just slowly slides his pinky finger up and down the inseam of my jeans on my inner thigh, effectively distracting me from our impending doom.

"It's going to be fine, baby," his deep voice rumbles over the sounds of the highway as we slow through traffic.

"Sure," I mumble.

"I mean it, Claire," Wes warns. I have learned that he doesn't appreciate my anxiety when it comes to our families and this wedding.

"Uh huh," I neither agree or disagree.

"Claire," he growls to get my attention.

"What?"

"Don't. Run."

"I'm not—" I start.

"I mean it," he takes a deep breath to calm himself. I like that he takes a moment to speak calmly when we both know that we're prone to short fuses and hot-blooded moments.

"I—" I start to deny it.

"Don't. Run," he enunciates. "Do not run from me. Do not run from us. I know that this is all scary for you but it's going to be okay. Don't run."

"Would you let me talk!" I snap.

"Yes."

"I'm not going to run." He quirks a brow in my direction. "I mean it! I know that I have run from you, from us, before but I have worked through that. I'm here now and I'm not going anywhere."

"You sure?" he asks. "You look like you have passports and plane tickets in mind."

"And I do." I shrug. "Sort of. I was thinking we should elope in Vegas and tell everyone afterwards. On a postcard." At that Wes throws his head back and laughs

"Let me get this straight," he rumbles. "You're not thinking of running from me, but you're planning on running away with me?"

"Yes." I nod.

"You don't have that deer-in-the-headlights look because of me but more because of your mom?"

"Yes," I answer. "Well, not as much Mom as Gran. She's scary." He chuckles at my response.

"What are you talking about? Your grandmother is a sweet old lady." I stare at him wide eyed. He can't be serious. Jesus Fucking Christ, he is.

"She just wants you to think that!" I'm practically shouting. "She's freaking crazy. And a little mean."

"You're kidding." Wes looks over at the serious expression on my face. "You're not kidding. You're really afraid of her. Holy shit, you're not afraid of anything to the point that you scare the shit out of me, and you're afraid of a ninety year old woman who can't even hit five feet tall on her tippy toes."

"You just wait," I warn him shaking my finger in his face. "Once you're officially family she'll be barking at you like she does the rest of us. You won't be off limits anymore because you're Lee's friend. You'll be digging ditches to hide the bodies like the rest of us."

"You don't really hide bodies, do you?" he asks. "Because I'm a federal agent and all that."

"Meh," I shrug. "Semantics."

"Uhh . . . no, it's not 'semantics' it's not something that's going to happen," he says before snapping his mouth shut. "You know what? You're stressed out and anxious about planning this wedding and I'm not going to let you scare me with a sweet, little old lady that I have known my entire life."

"Sure thing." I shrug. "Whatever you say."

Wes growls but before he can come back with something witty or extremely obnoxious we're turning onto the street that my parents have lived on for as long as I can remember. He has to park on the street because the driveway is filled with the vehicles owned by everyone we have ever known—Lee's Tahoe that's an upgrade from mine, it must be good to be the king, Anna's merc, and Emma's Mazda 3. Not to mention the Cadillac my grandmother has been driving since the 90's and the O'Connell's BMW. My nephew's vintage Charger rounds out the ensemble cast.

My late half-sister Bonnie's kids are the bright spot in all of our lives. We never would have known that any of them existed, our sister included, if she hadn't been murdered by a serial killer two months ago. Since her ex-husband had pulled a runner years earlier, her kids now live with my parents who had petitioned the court for custody and won recently.

Wes steps out of the car and comes around to open the door for me. He holds his hand out for me and I take it, letting him pull me from the car. He keeps hold of my hand in his as we walk across the street and up the walk to my parents' front door.

I can hear the noise, laughter and voices, an overall huge commotion. It's wild, it's love, it's joy and sometimes sadness and hardship, but it's all ours. I stop on the walk outside my family home and close my eyes, not because I'm overwhelmed don't know how to handle it, but because I know how all to fleeting these moments can be. I want to make certain that I soak them all in while I can.

When I open my eyes again, Wes looks worried until I smile at him, showing him that I am truly happy. We don't knock on the door. This is our family and our family home. Wes having grown up as Liam's best friend spent almost as much time here as Lee and I did.

When we first walk in all conversation stops. We all stand there looking at each other wide-eyed until my Gran breaks the silence.

"Good, now we can get started." She claps her hands making it so.

"Oh shit," Wes whispers.

"See?" I snap a little hysterical. "I freaking told you so!"

"I may have been a little naive before . . ." he admits, and I can't help but laugh.

"Quick, you two, get in here," my mom waves her arms trying to hurry us into the dining room with everyone else. "Before she starts throwing my dishes."

"She won't really throw the dishes, will she?" Wes asks. I just shoot him a withering glare. I hope he's happy now.

"Marta and Claire, come help me set the table," my grandmother demands. "You too, hussies!"

"Gran!" I shout at the same time my mother shouts too.

"Deirdre! You can't just call people hussies," my mom chastises my grandmother. The two have an interesting relationship. Both women married into the Goodnite family, but my Gran seems to forget that part and has spent the last thirty-nine years telling my mom that she doesn't belong. It's a little awkward and more than a little hostile.

"Yeah," Emma agrees. "Claire was a way bigger hussy than I ever was." My brother chokes on his beer while Wes looks down right murderous. I need to get this train back on track and fast!

"Let's not get ahead of ourselves here. We're all family. Let's get the food on the table," I say as I clap my hands in a fake cheer.

"Yeah, okay," my friends grumble but follow me into the kitchen.

"Shut it on the whore calling!" I demand under my breath.

We all pitch in and carry platters of food. My mom and my grandmother went all out for this meal. They must have been cooking all day by the looks of it. Each platter is piled high with mashed potatoes, pork chops, macaroni, green beans, a huge wooden bowl filled with a freshly made salad, and a large basket with hot rolls fills every available nook and cranny of the table.

We all take our places around the table, my dad at the head with my mom at the other end. Lee and I sit on either side usually, but with the house full of people and my parents now raising three more children, our places have changed. Lee sits on one side of dad and

Eric, who is home on leave from the Army, sits on his other side. I sit next to my mom and Seth, who is the baby of the family at ten sits on her other side. Wes sits next to me and Gran on his other side, I snicker evilly at the prospect. Brooklyn, who is nineteen and studying social sciences at the local college sits next to Seth. The last to sit are Emma and Anna who are jockeying each other to *not* sit next to Lee whose face is turning a deeper and deeper shade of red as time goes by. While I enjoy watching him squirm, I can't let it go on too long.

"Oh shit," I say with obvious fake disappointment. "I forgot my wine in the kitchen."

I jump up and run into the kitchen before anyone can stop me. When I come back with it *and* the bottle in hand I snap my fingers like I had just remembered something important and set my bounty on the table in front of me, specifically, next to Lee. He is my brother after all . . . even if he is being a horse's ass right now.

"Lee, I need to update you on that missings case," I say sitting down in the seat next to Lee and shoving my friends out of the way with a just go with it smile on my face.

Everyone adjusts their seating accordingly. My dad looks at me approvingly. When I look over at Wes he smiles softly and shoots me a wink. These guys—my guys—they get me, and I love that. I love them, and I would do anything for them. Obviously.

Lee stretches his arm across the back of my chair before leaning in to whisper in my ear, "You're a good sister."

"Of course," I agree with a smile. "I love you, big

brother."

"I love you too, kid," he says, and I know that he means it. Lee can be hard on me, especially at work, but it's not for a lack of love. He would do anything for me and just wants to protect me.

Our dad clears his throat. "I think it's only fitting that Eric says grace while he's home. Son, if you will . . ."

"Y-yes, Sir," he says as he clears his throat, his eyes swim deep with emotion on his stoic soldier's face. Eric was away, stationed across the country in the Army when his mom, the half-sister Lee and I never knew we had, was murdered. Now, with his brother and sister, we're all one big family. These kids are Goodnites in everything but name. Especially their looks, sharing our black hair and violet eyes.

I just wish our little family could have included his mom while she was alive.

"Grandad," my dad softly corrects.

"Yes, Grandad," Eric says before having us all bow our heads. "Dear Lord, thank you for the food before us and the blessings we have received, but also for this family which you have blessed us with. Thank you for watching over Lee, Claire, and Wes so that they may do their duties—"

"And also, for watching out for our nephew, Eric," Lee adds softly.

"And for leading us home when we thought all was lost. Lastly, please watch over our mother as we know without a doubt she is in your house now. In Jesus name . . ."

"Amen," was said all around the table.

Everyone reaches for bowls and platters in front of them and then passing them to their left—as is the only way we do large family dinners. Everyone's plate is overflowing, forks are raised, and mouths are full, no doubt the way the old bird planned it. When she raises her glass and taps the tines of her fork to it, I narrow my eyes in her direction suspiciously. My grandmother just smiles an innocent smile that I know, without a doubt, is one hundred percent bullshit.

"I just wanted to let you all know that today while I was lighting a candle for your dearly departed grandfather and sister, I booked St. Michael's church for your wedding on October eighth," Gran says matter of factly. Everyone just sits there froze, staring on wide-eyed, no doubt the exact way she wanted it. "You're welcome. Now say 'thank you' like a good girl."

I might have growled. The noise was cut off when Lee kicked me under the table.

"I don't think Wes and I were planning on a church wedding, Gran," I say swallowing my nervousness. "But thank you for the offer. Also, October seems a little . . . fast."

"Well, I for one, think a church wedding is perfect," Mrs. O'Connell chimes in with a gleeful smile, obviously enjoying my being cornered and unhappy.

"Also," Gran wades in. "It's not too soon. If we give you too long, you'll run away again. You know, cold feet."

"Does everyone think I'm going to bolt?" I ask instantly regretting it when everyone looks at their plates awkwardly, except Wes, Wes just looks hurt.

"Claire—" my dad says my name.

"No!" I shout. "I think I'm done here." I push back from the table standing.

"Sit down, Claire," he orders and my inner twelve-year-old Claire has me do just that in true petulant fashion.

"I expected more from you all," I say softly. "I love you all and I thought you loved me."

"We do—" my mom starts but I don't let her finish.

"I love Wes and I'm not going anywhere, but I'm not real happy with any of you right now."

"I'm sorry, Sis," Lee says.

"Me too," Emma adds.

"Same," Anna says softly.

"Well, I don't really know you all that well, so you had my vote of confidence," Eric says from across the table. "Plus, you're a way better shot than the frog. Clearly, he's marrying up," he finishes shooting me and Lee a saucy wink. I love that kid so much and as I look at him, I realize that he's not a kid at all and we've missed all of it.

"Now that that's all out of the way," Gran adds and groans go up all around the table as everyone resumes eating dinner. "I also signed you up for marriage classes."

"What?" I shout. "I'm not going to more head shrinking!"

"Really?" Anna asks on a raised brow.

"You know what I mean!"

"I'm not sure that I do . . ." She shrugs.

"Anna . . . Emma . . . help me out here," I plead.

"Actually, I think it'll be good for both of you," Anna says. "Professionally speaking." I narrow my eyes at her.

"This isn't fair," I pout.

"Actually, I think it's great," Lee says on a wicked smile. "You're lucky to get to go to these classes," he says laying it on real thick.

"I'm glad you feel that way, Liam," Gran says, and I know this is going to be good. My smile splits my face and there is nothing I could do to stop it. "I signed you and the two trollups up for their singles group. Father Matthew has a great marriage success rate."

"Gran—" Lee warns.

"What?" she shrugs. "It's already done. Unless there's something else going on here I don't know about . . . You and the blonde would make beautiful babies."

"Nothing's going on," Emma barks looking irritated.

"Yeah, nothing to see here, Gran," Lee adds disappointed and poor Anna just looks so lost and sad. She's clearly losing her battle with her hope to let go.

"When do all of these classes start?" Lee asks on a sigh.

"Tomorrow at eight." She smiles triumphantly.

"I'm never getting married," Eric mumbles and my dad laughs.

"Yeah, me either," Seth agrees. "Girls are gross!"

"Well, that plan isn't working out so great for your uncle," Dad says to his plate. Lee just sighs again.

"I just love that new priest they have there," Mrs. O'Connell shares. "He's so young and insightful."

"I prefer Father Matthew," Gran says just to pick a fight. "He's been the priest at that church since my son was born."

"Well, maybe we need a change up for the wedding," Mrs. O'Connell says obviously feeling a need to come out the winner of this argument.

"We'll see," Gran says.

"I'm still not sure we agreed on a church wedding," I say to no one in particular.

"Didn't we, though?" Wes asks me with barely restrained laughter in his voice.

"So much for a united front," I grumble under my breath.

"I love these family dinners!" Wes says happily while Lee and I both plot his murder from across the table.

chapter 12

shit

"'*LET THERE BE NO SEXUAL immorality, impurity, or greed among you. Such sins have no place among God's people.' I had such high hopes for you and yet you were still a disappointment.*"

She blinks her eyes furiously and rolls her head side to side. The blow she took is clearly having an effect on her, but she won't suffer long. Our Lord is merciful tonight.

I pull the large hunting knife out of its sheath and trace it over her body. I let the blade skim her arms one by one. I offer up the gentlest caress of the tip along her pink cheek.

"P-p-please," she pleads with me. "D-d-d-don't d-d-do this."

"You, my dear, should have thought about that before you sinned."

"I-I-I didn't!" she cries.

"Fornication is a sin, Kerrigan. Didn't you listen to a word that I said?" I snap letting her big eyes get

to me. I try and remind myself that she is a child of God and therefore imperfect, but she listened to Lucifer and his silver tongue.

"I didn't. I'm a good girl." She looks away because we both know that it's a lie. Just last week I had caught her letting a man paw at her like a common whore. She was better than that. At least I had thought so before then. But I have been wrong in the past.

"I really wish you were, Kerrigan. Trust me, this hurts me more than you."

She starts fighting the ropes binding her wrists in earnest now, but it doesn't matter. It's too late for her. It'll all be over in a minute or two.

I take the hilt of the knife in both hands and raise it up over my heads before driving it down in between her breasts. My blade hits bone and a gurgling sound falls from her lying lips. I slide the knife free from her body and raise it again. I thrust it into her body over and over again until I am sure that she is gone.

And then I slide the tip just below the surface of her skin just below her collarbone, marking her with the letter A—adultery is the ultimate sin after all and I am doing the Lord's work.

The rest of the evening was fairly uneventful if one considers being run over by a truck over and over again uneventful, but hey, who am I to judge?

After Emma, Anna, and I clear the table, I help

Gran do the dishes. Emma slides in next to me at the sink with a dish towel and Anna armed with the same is on the other side.

"I guess I'll just go relax," Gran says with a huff before leaving the kitchen.

"She kind of scares me," Emma admits.

"Meh." I shrug. "She's a little mean but we love her."

"Awe, come on, she's not so bad," Anna laughs.

"Anna, she keeps calling us 'the trollops'. You can't tell me that you're okay with that," Emma challenges.

"She only has the power over me that I give her."

"Bullshit," Emma snaps.

"It's true," Anna tells us. "You're letting it get to you. Just ignore it."

"Don't you head shrink me!" Emma barks and Anna visibly shrinks back. As it turns out, Emma is one of the few who Anna gave that power to.

"I'm sorry," she says in a little voice that makes my stomach roll. I hate that this strong, confident woman has been reduced to feeling so very small and insignificant.

"Anna—" Emma starts.

"No, you're right. Let's just forget it," Anna says softly.

"Anna—" Emma starts again.

"I said I just want to forget it." Anna rolls her shoulder back mustering up the courage and I can't help but feel like when she said she didn't belong with us that that was only the tip of the iceberg. "So how ugly of a bridesmaid dress are you making us wear? What are our color options?"

"I'll literally wear anything but pink," Emma chimes in taking the hint and following the subject change no matter how abrupt.

"What?" Anna shrieks. "No! I love pink."

"Why am I not surprised?" Emma sighs.

"Pink it is!" I cheer enthusiastically. That's what Emma gets for being an ass to Anna. I'm the only one that gets to be an asshole to her. For years, Anna has been hounding me to fix my shit, first in an official capacity and now as one of my closest friends. She's been kicking my ass for years, but building me back up at the same time. So, I'm a little protective of her. If anyone is going to kick her ass it's going to be me and only in the nicest of ways.

We are just heading into the living room to settle in for coffee and cake when my phone rings. I pull it out of my back pocket wondering who would be calling me since everyone I know is currently under this roof. Shit, it's probably the station.

"Goodnite," I answer.

"*Detective Goodnite, this is dispatch,*" they inform me. "*I have officers who have responded to a body in an alleyway.*"

"I'm not the on-call Detective tonight, dispatch," I inform them of what they should already know. "I believe Juarez is tonight."

"*I'm sorry, Detective, it's been a long day. The victim matches the description of your missing person. I should have led with that and I'm sorry.*"

"Next time," I say. "Where is this alley?"

"*A body was found behind the Pig & Chicken on*

the corner of Fourth and Main."
    "I'm on my way."

chapter 13

no fucking way

"**HEY, BABY, YOU GOIN'** my way?" Wes asks as he twirls his keys around his finger. I roll my eyes but smile anyways.

"Yeah," I say, my voice a little breathy. Plus, I don't have a car here.

"Then let's go," he offers while holding out his hand for me to take and like I always will, I do.

"Well, duty calls," I shout into the crowded room.

"I take it you gotta live one?" Dad asks.

"Nope, I got an *un*-live one," I laugh at my own joke. My dad just rolls his eyes at me.

"You got a body?" Lee asks.

"Yep." I nod my head looking him in the eyes, so he knows what I'm not saying out loud.

"The missing persons?" he asks me.

"Yeah, it's looking that way," I confirm.

"Damn." Lee shakes his head and with all that's going on with Lee, Emma, and Anna, I forget that a long time ago, Kerrigan meant something to him too so he will feel this one on a much deeper level.

"You said it," I sigh.

Wes and I stop to kiss everyone goodbye before heading out the door. He takes my hand in his and leads me across the street before pulling open my door for me. I climb in as he closes the door behind me before rounding the car and climbing in the driver's seat. Wes cranks the engine before leaning over and asking me, "Where to, Detective?"

"The Pig & Chicken on Fourth and Main," I tell him before adding, "And step on it."

Wes pulls away from the curb and heads towards the crime scene behind the Pig and Chicken. The bar isn't far from where my parents still live. George Washington Township is large in population but small in actual territory. Even though it should only take five minutes to get somewhere, with traffic and stop lights, it will probably take about twenty minutes on a good day.

"There's the ambulance," Wes says as he drives down Second Avenue. "Think we're in the right place."

"Shit," I mutter to myself. I always hope the call is wrong until I get there and see it for myself with my own two eyes. The ambulance behind the bar tells me that Kerrigan Adams is most likely dead, but then again, I always knew that she probably was.

Wes cuts the engine and we climb from the vehicle. Here I don't wait for Wes to open my door and he doesn't dote on me non-stop. Here we're a Federal Agent and a Detective, the fact that we go to the same house at the end of the night has nothing to do with the case and the facts.

I approach the crime scene tape and the officer guarding against civilian intruders and looky-loos. I pull my badge off my pocket and hold it up to view.

"Detective Goodnite, we've been waiting for you," the officer interrupts me.

"Show me what you got, Officer."

He lifts the bright yellow crime scene tape up for me to slip underneath, letting it drop back down into place after I pop up on the other side. Wes follows me through.

"Agent O'Connell, to what do we owe this visit?" the officer asks.

"I'm with her," Wes tosses a thumb over his shoulder towards me.

"I had heard something about that," the officer adds. "I can't believe the good Detective fell for your shit hook, line, and sinker."

"Yep," Wes adds with a ridiculous smile. "I finally wore her down."

"She seems too smart to get tangled up with the likes of someone like you," the officer laughs letting me know that Wes and this guy go way back, and I won't have to kick some ass tonight to defend my man's honor. And I would if I had to.

"Thanks for the vote of confidence, Rodriguez," Wes sighs.

"There's a crime scene, ladies," I roll my eyes at these two idiots. "Could we get back to that, please?"

"Oh, right. Sorry, Detective Goodnite," Officer Rodriguez says duly chastised.

"It's fine," I say.

"The victim appears to be mid to late thirties, brown

hair and brown eyes," he rattles off the facts. This is what I need right now—just the facts—as he leads us around the corner to where the crime scene technicians are photographing the scene and taking samples. "The responding detective said you were looking into a missing persons this morning. Could it be her?"

"It's possible. Is CSU running fingerprints?" I ask.

"They are but it can take awhile. You know how it is." He shrugs his meaty shoulder.

"I do. Who found her?" I ask him.

"The bartender came out to toss some trash in the dumpster and there she was," he answers.

"Overdose? Slip and fall? How did she buy it? Do we know?" I ask.

"Uhh . . . no," he says vaguely. "It's one of those things that you just have to see for yourself."

"Well, what happened?" I ask as I become frustrated with vague, half answers.

"She was stabbed to death," he says bluntly.

We round the corner just in time to get a quick glimpse of the crime scene and it was surprisingly clean of blood and gore for a stabbing. It's easy to assume that she was done somewhere else and moved here.

This isn't so bad. Maybe a mugging gone wrong . . . I just start to think that this might be a fairly easy case when I realize all those sayings about counting chickens and eggs in baskets is sadly correct.

It's not until we get closer that I realize just how wrong my original assessment was. A dark-haired woman who I can't help but believe that the tests will come back as Kerrigan Adams, is sitting up against the wall just outside the back door to the Pig & Chicken. Her legs are stretched out in front of her and her ankles are crossed. Her head is slumped forward and red slashes crisscross all over her exposed skin and torn clothes.

But the most remarkable item that my brain seems to latch onto is the giant letter A carved into her exposed chest. It's not carved neatly enough to know for sure. Maybe it's just a bunch of randomly placed stab wounds. I don't know. Only time with Emma in her morgue will tell.

"No fucking way," Wes thunders from behind me. "Absolutely not."

"It's not your choice, Wes," I say firmly. "This is my job."

"The hell it isn't!" he thunders. "I have a say in your safety."

"This was my case from the beginning. I have to see it through," I explain.

"No, you do not. You've had this case for all of twelve hours. Let someone else take it."

"No," I tell him. "It's mine and I'm keeping it."

"I'll take it and pass it on to one of my agents," he explains with a self-satisfied gleam in his eyes.

"I don't think so!" I shout back. "This case is mine."

"I can't do this again, Claire," Wes pleads. "Please."

"Don't make me choose, Wes." It's not fair. Just when I think my life is finally becoming something good, something decent, someone or something is taken from me. Well, not anymore.

"Right back at you, babe," he snaps. It lands like a blow to my chest. "You think, for even one fucking second, that I want to sit back and watch you chase down some sicko again? You think I want to watch you die?"

"That's not going to happen," I try to say.

"Can you guarantee that?" he asks.

"No."

"I didn't think so," Wes snaps.

"Wes—" I start but he cuts me off.

"Don't. Don't even finish that sentence," he roars.

"Please," I plead, and I hate it. This isn't the place to be having an argument and yet, here we are, behaving about as unprofessional as you can get.

"I'm not going to ask you to pick me over this case, over your job, whatever you're working yourself up about in your head. I already know how that will play out and it's not good for anyone." He shakes his head sadly before looking me in the eyes again. "But I am asking you to think of me, *even just a little*, when you make your decision. Until then, I'll stay out of your way."

"Wes, don't do this," I plead softly.

"Let me know what you decide."

And then he turns on his heel and stalks off into the night. I let out a heavy sigh. Wes is right. I do need to consider his feelings, but Kerrigan also needs to find justice. He's right, I have a big decision to make. I should probably walk away from this case. Until then, we'll just have to wait to see what the morning brings . . .

chapter 14

no dice

SHIT!

There's nothing I can do right now, and I hate that. Wes has gone home—to our home—the home we share together because three weeks ago I let my shitty apartment go once and for all. In reality, it's his home and always will be if he walks away from me.

Not a fucking chance.

For all the running that I did and the chasing Wes did, I am not letting him walk away without a fight. Too damn bad. No dice. We're engaged. I wear a ring the size of Rudolph's red nose—*his ring*—on my left hand. Our families are planning the most ostentatious wedding this side of the Hudson. He is not going to run from me.

I do, however, have to interview this bartender and follow up with the scene before turning it over to another detective. That means sticking around here until the wee hours of the morning and then crawling home to shower and hold onto Wes like my life depends on it.

That is going to prove more difficult that I had originally thought because I don't have a car. I do have house keys though, so I can still get in. Wes is mad, but he would never lock me out. The hurt and the fear that flashed in his whiskey eyes cut me to the quick. He's got his back up because he's scared, and not for himself, but for me.

No, Wes isn't ready to walk away, to throw in the towel on us, but he is asking me to pick him, and that is exactly what I'm going to do. When I think of all the things I have put Wes through over the last year, really the last thirty, he needs me to choose him. He has stuck by me through everything. Every little thing and not so little thing. It's time I stood by him too. I pull my phone out of my pocket and dial the one number I know I need to right now.

"Hey, Sis, what's up?" Lee answers after the first ring.

"I have a situation, think you can come down here and help a gal out?" I ask my big brother for a favor.

"Thank you, Jesus," he mumbles in the background. Clearly things haven't been all sunshine and roses at Casa Goodnite since Wes and I left for the homicide. "I'll be right there. Where are you?"

"I'm in the alleyway behind the *Pig & Chicken* on the corner of Fourth and Main."

"I know exactly where that is." Of course, he does. My trampy brother knows all the bars around town. Where else would he pick up all of his ladies of right now? The exact ones that got him in this predicament with my two best friends. *My only two friends*. I could just kill him sometimes.

"See you soon," I say before ending the call.

I walk back over to the door to the bar where the officer is waiting for me. He gives me a wary look after witnessing the entire embarrassing ordeal with Wes and then my calling my brother for help. I let out a heavy sigh before pressing forward. My street cred as a crazy badass is going to be sorely lacking after this.

"Let's go talk to the bartender," I say as he lifts the tape up for me one more time.

"Sure thing, Detective." He does not say another word. He does not comment on all that he's seen or voice his opinion. He will never know how much I truly appreciate that in this moment.

We push through the back door of the bar, careful not to disturb the crime scene. The bar is empty, having been shut down shortly after the body was discovered. Only low overhead lights are still on giving the room an eerie glow.

The officer leads me down a small hallway off of the back of the building towards an office. The bright fluorescent lights leak out of the partially closed doorway. I knock on the door jamb.

"Come in," a gruff voice says.

I push open the door and see a man about my age with a decent build, slumped over his desk with his face in his hands. I can't really blame him. Seeing a murder victim like that changes you and never for the good.

"I'm Detective Goodnite," I say introducing myself. "I'd like to ask you a few questions."

"Good," he says with his voice muffled by his arms. "I'd like to answer those questions and then fall deep down into a bottle of bourbon." And again, I can't blame him. Sometimes that's my own answer to the nightmares that plague me even if it's not completely healthy and Anna would cringe.

When he looks up and lets his eyes meet mine I see the shock in them. I am almost certain that this man had nothing to do with the appearance of Kerrigan Adams's body in the back alley behind his bar.

"Would you please tell me, in your own words, what happened tonight?"

"It was about eight and there was a lull in the crowd. It's never really busy on a Monday night anyways. Everyone is still recovering from the weekend. But I took the opportunity to take the trash out."

He pauses, taking a deep breath before continuing. I don't stop him. He obviously needs to regain a little bit of his composure.

"When I opened the door, I didn't see her." He runs his hand through his hair and I watch it shake. "The dumpster is straight out the door and I didn't see her. I had my back to her. But when I turned around, there she was, leaning up against the wall."

"What did you do then?" I ask.

"I touched my fingers to her throat looking for a pulse, but I knew. I looked in her opened eyes and just knew that I wouldn't find one. That was when I saw the . . . the marks on her torso and . . ."

"And what?" I ask.

"I threw up in the alley and then called 9-1-1." Most people do when they see a dead body for the first time and this one was particularly gruesome, so I don't blame him.

"Did you stay with her out there or did you go back inside?" I ask him.

"I went back inside to tell the assistant bartender to man the bar while I was waiting for the cops."

"And then what did you do?" I ask.

"I told them everything I just told you and showed them where she was when they showed up. When they told me to clear out the bar, I did. And when they told me to wait inside I came in here."

"Have you ever seen that woman here before?" I press on.

"No, but it's a busy bar. She could be in often and I wouldn't know if she's not someone I'm looking for, you know?"

"She's not your type," I surmise.

"She's not batting with the right equipment." He smiles cheekily before remembering what had happened to her behind his bar and letting his smile slip off his handsome face.

"Gotcha," I say. "Thank you for your time. If I need anything else, I'll let you know."

"Thanks," he says quietly.

"Enjoy the bourbon. Do you need someone to get you home safely?" I ask him.

"No, I think I'll take it to go," he says while looking me in the eyes and I believe him. I breathe a sigh of relief knowing that we won't be scraping him off of a tree or a guardrail later tonight because he couldn't deal with what he saw here and decided to combat that experience with booze before climbing behind the wheel of a vehicle.

"Good," I say before heading back out into the

hallway.

I push back through to the door and out into the alleyway. The body has been moved, probably taken to the morgue where Emma will get to work on her in the morning. Tonight, her technicians will get me a positive fingerprint ID before moving on.

The most exciting find is that Lee is there and looking very relieved to be at a crime scene at ten in the evening.

"Well, if it isn't the prodigal son." I smirk.

"What do you have, Goodnite?" he asks. "I didn't come here to be harassed. For that I could have stayed at Mom and Dad's place."

"Things still rough with the ladies?" I ask.

"She hates me," he says on a sigh.

"She does," I agree.

"She took every opportunity after you left to call me an asshole in the most poignant ways."

"I'm not surprised, and you shouldn't be either. Honestly, what did you expect, Lee?" I ask letting my frustration seep into my voice.

"Not to fall in love with her," he says so quiet I almost didn't hear him.

"Excuse me, Detective," one of the officers interrupts. "We have a positive ID on the victim confirmed as Kerrigan Adams."

"Thank you," tell him.

"Has she been transported yet?" Lee asks the officer.

"Yes, Sir. The body mover just left with her," Officer Rodriguez informs us.

"Thank you," Lee also tells him. "Detective Goodnite and I will make the notification call to her next of kin."

"Yes, Sir," he says before leaving.

"Shall we?" Lee asks me.

"Yeah," I sigh.

We head down the alleyway to where his own SUV is waiting and climb in. Lee starts the engine and heads back towards our childhood home. He pulls over at the curb in front of the Adams's home.

"You ready?" he turns to ask me before we step out of the car.

"I never am."

"Me either," he sighs.

"Let's get it over with then," I say as the digital clock on the dash flips to midnight.

The walk up to their front door has my stomach turning in knots. Lee rings the doorbell and we stand there and wait. When the porch light flips on a calm rolls over me and a steel climbs up my spine. This is my job and I will do it well. This is my duty to them and their daughter and I will see it carried out.

The front door opens and Mr. Adams takes one look at me before calling up the stairs, "You better come on down, Molly."

He nods pushing open the front door but doesn't say anything to Lee or me. We follow him inside to the living room, Mrs. Adams is standing there in her robe and nightgown. When she sees me her face crumples and she begins to cry. Mr. Adams moves to her pulls her into his arms. Lee and I stand there giving them a moment before I give them the words we all hoped I never would.

"This is Captain Goodnite," I say pointing to Lee.

"I remember you," Mr. Adams says to him. "You had the biggest crush on our Kerry and she wouldn't give you the time of day, poor boy."

"That's true," Lee says with a soft smile playing about his mouth as he takes a walk down memory lane.

"I always liked you. Thought you treated her with kindness and respect even when she didn't deserve it," Mike Adams shares.

"I try," Lee says softly.

"She must be your sister," he says nodding towards me.

"She is," Lee confirms.

"Last I saw of her she was an itty-bitty thing. I didn't put two and two together when she was here earlier, but I see it now. You should be proud of her," he says to Lee.

"I am, Sir," Lee says, and I can hear the truth in his words. Despite the spike in blood pressure I cause him on a daily basis, Lee *is* proud of me.

"Thank you," I say softly.

"I'm ready now," he says looking me in the eyes. "Tell me what you can here to say."

"Mr. Adams, it is with our deepest sympathies that we have come here to inform you that the body of your daughter, Kerrigan Adams, has been recovered this evening," Lee says in his modest but commanding tone of voice.

"No!" Mrs. Adams cries but Mr. Adams looks on, I think he always knew this was the ending they would get. Stand up people like Kerrigan don't just run off one day.

"Was it an accident?" he asks.

"No, Sir," Lee answers.

"Can you tell me what happened?" he asks.

"Not at this time due to pending investigation but you need to know that your daughter was murdered," Lee says softly.

"What?" he cries. "Who would do this? My Kerry is a good girl!"

"I don't know," Lee says. "But we're going to find out."

Shit! I think. I never got around to telling him I need off this case. Fuck! How am I going to do that now? The web of my life is twisting tighter and tighter. Something tells me that before it's all said and done, I'll realize that I have made a terrible mistake.

It's after one in the morning by the time Lee pulls up in front of our home.

"You gonna be okay, kid?" Lee asks me just as I reach for my seatbelt to climb out of the SUV.

"Of course," I answer. "Why wouldn't I be?"

"I heard about the fight," he says, his voice low but it still resonates in the dark car.

"I don't know what you're talking about," I lie.

"You do," he presses on. "Wes freaked out when he saw the body and demanded that you choose between him and the case."

I pause hoping that the right response will pop into

my head, but truthfully, I'm too freaking tired to come up with anything that will remotely sound plausible. When I open mouth with the intent to just let anything fall out, Lee stops me in my tracks.

"Don't even bother lying to me."

"Fine," I snap. "We fought. It was unpleasant. He left. End of story."

"You need off this case," he surmises. This might be my opening. I might be able to get Lee to let me off this case easy. But I need to tread lightly because it's Lee and because he can be an ass sometimes.

"I don't," I say denying the truth of it.

"You do," Lee presses.

"I do." I sigh.

"We're loaded down with cases department wide. I'll do my best, but I can't make any guarantees." Yes, I am getting off this case. Lee is going to help me out and I am so relieved.

"Just try," I plead.

"I will," my brother promises me.

"Thanks, Lee." I smile at him and I really appreciate his willingness to help me out of this tight spot. It makes me feel like everything is going to be just fine and I had nothing to worry about. Now, I need to get upstairs to be with my guy, *my forever guy*.

"Anything for you, kiddo."

"I hate when you call me that," I tell him making a smile tug at the corner of his lips. It makes him seem younger, softer, a little less rough around the edges even. I can see why both of my best friends are in love with him.

"I know." He laughs. That ass.

"And there you go, you just had to ruin the moment," I say as I push open the car door.

"I'll talk to him and try to explain things," Lee offers.

"He'll just think it's an excuse on my part to have my cake and eat it too." By the look on his face Lee knows that I'm right. It'll blow up in both of our faces and cost us both having Wes in our lives. That's not something I am willing to risk for either of us. Not now, not ever.

"Okay, your call. Just let me know," he says before I close the door and head up the front walk.

The house is totally dark. There is not light welcoming me home on the front porch, no lights left on in the front of the house, down the hall, or up the stairs. The sight is chilling. Above all I can't help but think that Wes didn't expect me to come home, he didn't expect me to choose him.

I climb the stairs in the dark, walk straight down the hall, and through our bedroom into the closet. I lock my sidearm and my drop gun into the small safe and pull of my boots letting them fall to the closet floor. I shimmy out of my jeans and do that bra pull through trick that junior high girls do to change in the locker room and drop my bra on the floor with everything else.

I pad my way back into the bedroom in nothing but panties, my t-shirt, and a pair of tall socks because Wes runs so hot the air conditioning is always set to arctic tundra. When I look at him, he's sound asleep. Wes doesn't even know that I'm home and I'm so afraid to tell him that I'm not officially off of the case that I don't want to wake him only to make up some lame excuses.

I pull the comforter and sheet back as gently as possible before climbing in. I roll over and wrap my arms around Wes, my front to his back with my forehead pressed to the center of his back. He does not move. With him safely asleep and oblivious to me I feel like I can finally pour my heart out, so I do.

"I love you Wes. With my whole heart, I love you. I talked to Lee tonight and he's going to do the best that he can to get me off of the Adams case. I know you won't believe me when you hear it, but it's true. This is me picking you. You told me to make up my own mind and it's you. I love you and this is me choosing you."

I thought I felt his body tighten under mine just a smidge but then it was gone. I close my eyes and hope to God that in the morning everything will be right again, that the sinking feeling in the pit of my stomach is nothing. But as I drift off into sleep I don't see that Wes wasn't asleep and not only didn't believe me, but that he was very, very disappointed in me. That maybe I should have realized that my gut is never wrong.

chapter 15

*"**C**OME OUT OF THE closet, baby."*

"No," I whisper, tears hot on my face and snot stuffing up my nose.

Liam and Wes were right, I'm just a baby. A big kid wouldn't be crying in the dark corner of a closet hoping it'll all go away if you just wish hard enough. I bet Wes never cries. I know Lee doesn't.

"Come out now, Claire. Playtime is over."

"No," I cry louder. "Please don't make me."

"Now!" He growls as the closet door rattles. I gasp.

"Leave me alone!"

"Get out of the fucking closet, Claire!" he roars.

"Please no," I cry harder, my body shaking with each sob.

"When," he kicks his hard boots against the closet door and it shudders.

"Please."

"Are you." He kicks it again.

The doors are the kind with the slats that fold side-ways. We have them at home and mama says I always pinch my fingers in the accordion. Whatever that is.

"I just wanna go home," I whisper.

"Gonna," he kicks again.

"I just want my mommy," I sob. "Please. I just want my mommy." I want my family. I want my mommy and daddy, I want my brother and Wes.

"Fucking," the boards snaps and I scream.

"I just wanna go home, please," I beg. Lee and Wes wouldn't kick at me like this. Why does the man hate me? Why is he being so mean? I just don't know. I don't know why.

"Learn!" he shouts as he kicks the broken boards out of the way. He leans down and grabs me by my upper arms.

"Please," I wheeze but my words are cut short when he slaps my face hard. So hard I taste blood in my mouth and it's so yucky I feel sick. I'm going to throw up from the yucky taste. I try as hard as I can not to. I know that if I do, he'll punish me again. I don't want that. Anything but that.

"You are home, baby," he coos right before he slaps me again. I cry out again, falling to the floor with his last hit. It's so strong he knocks me down with it. "And I thought I told you to call me daddy," he says as he lands a hard kick to my back.

"You're not my daddy, you'll never be my daddy," I whisper. "My daddy is a nice man. He would never hurt me. You'll never be my daddy," I say again but the bad man can't hear me, he already walked away.

I have nowhere to go except back into the closet,

but one thing is for sure, no one will ever hit me or hurt me again. I'm going to make sure of it.

I wake with a resolve that I have never felt before.

For the first time in my life, my priorities are in order. Before I felt like I had nothing to keep me going but my job, which I love, but that wasn't entirely true. My job was all I had allowed in. But not anymore.

Now, I realize that the scope of my world is broader. I have my job and it's amazing, fulfilling, everything I could want, but I also have my family now without the barriers of my struggles between us. There are no more secrets. Because of that, Lee and I have a better relationship than ever. He no longer threatens to fire me every week and we work together well as part of a larger team.

I also have let in friends, for the first time in my adult life. When Anna started as my department shrink, I didn't trust her. I didn't believe that she had my best interests at heart, but now, I see that she has always had my best interests at heart. Even when that went against what Lee was paying her for. She has become my anchor in the fog of my broken memories, she's my voice of reason when I need it. And Emma, once just a colleague, is now my truth. She keeps me grounded but also pushes me when I need it. Emma with her brash tone and unvarnished opinions keeps life interesting. Both are totally opposite in every way and yet, I love them both equally. The sisters of my heart.

But with all this knowledge, with all of the people that my world includes, the center of that is and if I'm being honest with myself, has always been Wes. He has protected me and loved me, encouraged me and been by my side from the moment he realized this was our time. The only time we were ever going to get. We couldn't go backwards, but we can go forward.

It's time that I offer Wes the same unconditional love that he shows me.

I roll over to wrap him in my arms and tell him how much that I love him, to reassure him that everything is going to be alright, and to share with him the words I gave to him when he was asleep. But when I reach for him all I encounter is cold sheets and the stark realization that without a kiss goodbye or even a word, Wes is gone. Wes is gone from our bed, from our home, and I can't help the overwhelming feeling of being left behind.

This can be nothing but bad.

chapter 16

A DARK CLOUD HOVERS over me as I step into the shower—alone.

It wasn't long after I had realized that Wes was gone that I had lost it. I completely lost it. When my hand encountered nothing but cold sheets, I clutched his pillow in my grasp and pulled it into my chest. The warm, woodsy scent that belongs exclusively to Wes still clung to the gray cotton and I buried my face in its pillowy softness and inhaled deeply.

And then I promptly burst into tears.

I let myself bawl for what felt like years, but in reality was only thirty minutes or so. Then I pushed myself up to sit on the edge of the bed, letting my feet hang over the side. I reached over to the bedside table and picked up my phone, dialing the one number who would never turn me away.

"Hello?" she answered. It's early still and I can hear the sleep still clinging to her smoky voice.

"Hey, Anna," I hurried to continue, not bothering

to take a breath for fear that the words I need to say will choke me. That I will chicken out and refuse to say them. "It's me. I think I screwed up."

"Now why every would you think that?" she asked.

I wiped my eyes and sighed. "Because I did."

"How?" she said softly, ever the shrink our Anna is, always making me do all the talking while she only asks a question here and there.

"When we got to the crime scene last night," I explained. "It wasn't just a robbery gone bad . . . it was more."

"How so?" she asks me.

"A stabbing, a bad one," I answered.

"Well, that can't be out of the realm of possibility for a detective and a federal agent, can it?" she asks.

"Not normally, no . . ."

"But?" she asked, "Why do I feel like there is more?"

"Because there always is." I let out a weary sigh. "She was leaning up against the wall of the bar. Left there and there were these markings carved into her body. I couldn't see what," I described.

"I take it that she's your missing person?"

"Yes."

"Then what happened?" she asked.

"Wes took one look at her and the way she was dropped at the scene and freaked out," I explain. "I told him it wasn't his choice what I do with my career. While usually that would be correct, I can't help but feel like in this instance, I was wrong. But he just made me so mad!"

"Can you blame him?" she asked me.

"No," I groaned. "No, I can't. But we fought any-ways."

"What did you fight about?" she asks me.

"He told me to drop the case," I say. "He told me he wasn't going to stick around and watch me die at the hands of another serial killer."

"Did you?" she asks. "Drop the case, I mean."

"Not at all . . . at least not at that moment. I was too mad at being ordered around at a scene," I admit embarrassed.

"Then what happened?" she questions.

"He got so mad, Anna," I whispered feeling the tears sting the back of my eyes again. "He told me—*in front of everyone*—that he knew I wouldn't choose him and then he left."

"And what did you do?" she had asked me.

"I called Lee for help. He showed up after I had talked to the bartender and we waited for a positive ID on the victim, which we now have. Lee and I went and informed the next of kin, which was awful. Then he drove me home."

"And how was Wes when you got home?" Anna asks.

"Asleep." By now the tears are streaming down my face unchecked. I sniffle. "He didn't leave on any wel-coming lights, Anna."

"Welcoming lights?" she asked. "I'm not sure I un-derstand you."

"He didn't leave on the porch light or the hall light or the one in the living room!" I shout panicking. "He didn't even leave on a bathroom light. Anna, Wes didn't think I was coming home to him, but I did. I had told Lee I couldn't work this case anymore. That I had to choose Wes."

"And what did Lee say?"

I sigh. "He said the department was stretched too thin right now and that he couldn't spare me but that he would try."

"I'm beginning to think he might be a bit of the ass Emma swears he is," she had mumbled but I just kept going, lost in my freak out.

"But when I climbed into bed, I had told him everything. I told him how much I love him and that I'm choosing him, that I will always choose him."

"And what did Wes say?"

"Nothing. He was asleep," I tell her.

"Claire—" Anna starts to warn me, but I cut her off.

"I know!" I bite my lip. "I told you I screwed up and I know it now. I thought I had time. But I didn't because when I woke up this morning, he was gone!"

"Maybe it's not as bad as you think . . ." she tries.

"He was gone, Anna, as in not in this fucking house!" I shout.

"Okay," she tried again. "Let's just take this one minute at a time. Okay?"

"Okay," I say taking a deep breath.

"Now, go get dressed. Go to work. Tell Lee to pull his head out of his ass. And call Wes and talk to him about it. All of it," Anna orders me about.

"Okay. I can do that," I say feeling much better for having a plan. Anna always knows how to calm me down when I'm freaking out.

"I know you can and honey?" she tells me and

there's an encouraging kindness in her voice when she speaks to me like this that I treasure.

"Yeah?" I question.

"Everything will be fine."

And I mostly believed her as I showered and dressed for work in the early morning dark of the closet, but a dark cloud still hangs over me. I eat my bowl of cereal as quickly as I can before rinsing the bowl. It tastes like ash in my mouth. I pull my car keys off the hook by the door and realize I don't have a car because my department vehicle is once again at the station and I'm here.

"Fantastic," I mumble to myself as I pull my phone out of my pocket and order an Uber.

I push the glass front door of the station with a scowl on my face and my sunglasses covering my eyes. There is very little makeup on my face. I didn't even try to cover the bags from a late night at a crime scene and then an early morning crying. At the time I was getting dressed, I didn't even have it in me to try. Now that I'm walking in and looking at the faces of everyone I work with who by now have heard the latest chapter in the Claire and Wes tale of woe, I'm kind of wishing I had expended the effort. When I sit down everyone will take one look at my naked face and know without a doubt, that I chose wrong.

I walk straight to the kitchenette and pour myself the world's largest cup of coffee. As I stand there, I actually consider pouring the whole carafe into my mouth but I'm pretty sure that's not going to help me. So, I chug half of my mug letting it burn on the way down and reveling in that hurt. I need it. I embrace it. And then I tuck it away for later.

I top off my mug and head to my desk with my head held high, looking straight ahead. I refuse to cower or look anyone in the eye until I've had significantly more coffee than I have already consumed. I have just lowered my ass into my rickety office chair when the phone on my desk rings.

"Goodnite," I answer.

"Get your ass down here," Emma barks. *"You're going to want to see this."*

"Good morning to you too, Sunshine," I gripe.

"Har-de-har-har," she calls.

"I'm coming."

"That's what he said," she cackles into the phone before hanging up.

I groan as I push myself back up and out of this death trap on spiny wheels and snatch my cup of coffee up off of my desk, taking it with me. I stomp through the bullpen to the elevator and stab the call button with my index finger.

It dings its arrival cheerily and I feel anything but, my mood is sinking quicker than a New York football season. Still, I climb into the tin box and hope for the best even though I know that it's a wasted effort.

The doors pop open and spit me out into Emma's evil lair.

"Well, look what the cat dragged in," she says with a smile on her face that I just can't deal with right now.

"Yep, I'm here. Now tell me why," I demand.

"Well aren't we just a little merry ray of fucking sunshine this morning." Emma looks at me with a keen eye. I'm not really wanting to rehash everything but I'm also planning on sticking with my resolutions as of last night. That means not alienating one of the few people in my life who tolerate me well. Plus, I already told Anna, so I might as well even the score.

"I take it you haven't been to the water cooler yet to hear all of the juicy office gossip." I sigh.

"Oh, I have. I just wanted to see your face while you try and deny it," she says casually.

"It's true," I concede.

"How much of it?" she asks.

"Probably all of it. What did you hear?"

"In short?" she asks me.

"That will do."

"That Wes lost his shit at a crime scene last night and demanded you step down from the case, which you promptly told him to put in his pipe and smoke it. He then told you he didn't expect you to choose him and he wasn't going to stick around to watch you be gunned down by another sicko so he left."

"Is that all?" I deadpan.

"Well, you're down here, asking about the case, looking like hammered horse shit, so I'm assuming you chose wrong and are suffering the consequences." She takes a deep breath before pressing on. "I thought you were smarter than that!"

"Thank you," I sigh. "And I am but Lee won't let me off the case until we have someone to take it. So, I'm stuck."

"I always knew he was a miserable asshole," she mumbles.

"And besides, you called me." I shrug my shoulder and wink at her.

"So what if I did?" she asks looking down her nose at me.

"Well, then what the hell am I doing here?" I laugh at Emma's ridiculousness. There is this air of fun and a little crazy about her that balances perfectly with the utterly awful shit we see on this job. It makes me appreciate her more every day. I'm glad she's my friend.

"Oh, right," she says. "I wanted to show you what I found when we cleaned the body," she tells me.

"You mean the weird markings?"

"Yep."

"Well, what are they?" I ask losing my patience.

"Not markings, an initial."

"Like letters?" I ask. Shit I was right. I was hoping against hope that this case wasn't going to be weird, but it looks like today isn't my day to get the things that I want and I'd bet five dollars that my magic eight ball would show me that tomorrow's outlook isn't going to be so good either.

"Yes, well, a letter. To be specific the letter A," she says showing where she has cleaned the wounds and now you can see that the initial isn't as deep as the other stab wounds. I think it's safe to say that this was done on purpose. *Fantastic*.

Emma lifts up the sheet that was covering the body of Kerrigan Addams and folds it down to cover her breast. Sure enough, there over her clavicle, it the letter A carved into her skin.

"That's gruesome," I say thinking my thoughts allowed.

"It is. No wonder Wes lost his mind," she muses.

"Yeah, something like that," I agree.

"Are you going to cut him some slack?" she asks me. "Or are you going to kill this love story before it ever has a chance?"

"When did you become such a romantic?" I ask.

"I'm not and don't change the subject," Emma warns me. "But it's different for you. You have a chance at the holy grail, the full package with a decent package and I don't want to see you piss it away."

"I'll cut him some slack when he gives me a chance to explain," I answer.

"What do you mean?"

"Your knight in shining fed suit left before I had a chance to talk to him this morning. He's clearly nursing a grudge." I can't help the sigh that slips from my lips and there's a stinging behind my eyes every time I think about waking up alone and without Wes.

"Can you blame him?"

"Probably not," I say before changing the subject. "Can you email me some pictures of the carvings?"

"Sure thing," she says. "Maybe he'll show tonight."

I let out a groan. "Fuck! I forgot all about marriage counseling."

"I'm sure it'll be great." She laughs.

"Can you fail marriage counseling on the first night?" I ask half seriously.

"Well if anyone can it'll be you," she laughs again. "But I'm mostly sure that you'll be alright. Probably."

"On that depressing note, I'm going back to work,"

I tell her.

I climb into the elevator and ride it back upstairs. As soon as the door opens Lee bellows my name from within his sanctuary.

"Goodnite!" Lee shouts from his office.

"Seriously, how does he do that?" I grumble as I stalk over to his doorway.

"Yes?" I ask as I push open his door.

"Sit down," he orders.

"I don't wanna. I'll stand thanks," I say going out of my way to behave like a brat because I had a shitty night and a worse morning. I'm not willing to add Lee's shit to that long list of very unfortunate events.

"Can you cut me some slack, please?" he asks.

"Probably not, but I suppose I could try."

"How magnanimous of you, Your Highness." He rolls his eyes.

"Thank you," I bow and Lee laughs. "So, what's up?"

"Do you have autopsy results?" Lee asks me.

"I do. Kerrigan was stabbed to death, probably not behind the bar and the letter A was carved into her chest post mortem."

"That's gruesome," he says.

I sigh. "It is."

"A lover maybe?" he adds his theories into the pot.

"Her parents and coworkers say she wasn't seeing anyone," I answer.

"She could have been keeping it quiet—"

"Lee," I begin. That asshole is going to fuck me over. I can just feel it.

"Claire," he answers. "There's no proof."

"Lee," I start again. "You promised."

"There is no evidence that this is a serial killer, Detective Goodnite," he barks.

"You promised!" I shout at him.

"As your commanding officer I am telling you that this is the case that you were assigned. You will follow orders." Lee squares off with me and I have never been more hurt by his actions and angry with him before. Including all the times he tried to fire me and give my cases to Wes.

"You can't be serious . . . Lee?" I ask, hating all the while how small and scared my voice sounds.

"As a fucking heart attack," he growls at me.

"You miserable asshole," I bark leaning forward and placing my palms on his desk.

"Watch yourself, Detective," he warns, his voice low. "You are treading on very thin ice."

"You are miserable and alone in a bed of your own making and you can't stand to see Wes and I happy. I never thought the day would come when you would sabotage something so special to me. Something that I finally have that is so good and so real, because you've become such a fucking prick," I say standing and making my way to the door.

"You could always leave you gun and badge on my desk and see your way out of my department, Detective," Lee threatens.

"You would just love that, wouldn't you?"

"It won't break my heart." He shrugs his shoulder.

"Be careful what you wish for, Captain," I say before walking out the door. It only takes one quick look to realize that everyone heard. Everyone, even Emma, is standing around all wearing sad expressions on their faces. Well, not Emma, she looks pissed? Maybe, disappointed? Definitely.

But I can't bother with that now. Now, I have work to do. But I'll regret that later too.

chapter 17

incompatible

I SPEND THE REST of the day going over case notes and tracking down witness statements all with the feeling of impending doom looming in front of me.

By the time five o'clock rolls around I am a nervous wreck. I grab my keys from my desk drawer after shutting down my geriatric computer and head out to the lot. I haven't seen or heard from Wes all day and now all I can think about is being stood up for marriage classes.

That would be my worst nightmare.

I push through the glass doors and out to where my Tahoe is waiting in the back of the lot. It's eerie out here and I can't help the shiver that wracks down my spine. My Gran would say someone just stepped on my grave. I certainly hope not.

I beep the locks with my key fob and climb in pulling the door firmly shut behind me and hitting the locks. I fire up the engine and head towards my family church. Or impending doom. Whichever comes first.

The drive isn't nearly long enough to get my head on straight, but it was just enough to allow me to work myself up even more. By the time I pull into the parking lot, I have convinced myself that Wes will be a no show.

I park in the first available space and climb out. I spot Lee on the steps of the church trying to talk to Emma who is ignoring him in favor of Anna. Oh Lee, how could you be so incredibly stupid? I hustle up the steps at ten minutes until the hour when all of our groups are meeting.

Anna takes one look at me and shakes her head in the negative. I let out a harsh sigh.

"He could still show . . ." Emma tries to make me feel better. My vision is floating again, and my nose is burning. Shit I don't want to cry in front of all of these people.

"Yeah," I say softly.

"Claire, I'm—" Lee starts but he's cut off by Wes running up the steps just as the priest opens the doors.

"Sorry I'm late," he says. "There was a pile up on the turnpike."

"Okay," I say softly as he places his hand on the small of my back guiding me into the sanctuary.

"We'll talk later," he says as he leans in, his lips to my ear for only me to hear. All of the hope I felt upon seeing him comes crashing down like a balloon with a hole in it. Maybe that's exactly what we are—a popped balloon.

"Okay," I say softly before I choke up.

"Who's ready for Tuesday Singles?" the young priest asks. "Well, come on inside!"

Anna and Emma follow directly behind the priest with Lee on their heels. There are a few more men lingering in the parking lot but I'm sure they'll make their way in soon. A gaggle of three women I have never met before—but their whole appearance screams man eater—follow Lee in like they just broke their Weight Watchers plan and he's a Krispy Kreme.

"I hope I get to sit next to him," one says.

"Don't worry about that," another chimes in. "He won't be single for long if I have anything to say about it."

"He looked pretty interested in the blonde," the third adds.

"Like I said, don't worry about it." And then they all follow him in cackling.

"Oh shit," I mumble more to myself than anyone.

"It's Lee's mistake to make, Claire," he warns. "You know that."

"I do," I agree. "But I don't have to like it.."

"Maybe it'll be good for him." Wes shrugs his shoulder. "Or maybe he'll fuck it up like we all think he will." I sigh.

"You're not helping," I whisper.

"I know." He sighs. Wes opens his mouth to say something else, but the older priest walks out of an office interrupting him.

"You must be Claire and Wesley."

"Yes, Father," we say in unison.

"Well, that's off to a good start," the priest jokes. If only he knew that it was all downhill from there. "Right this way."

We follow him back down a hall and into another

office when he motions for us to sit down in a pair of chairs facing a third chair.

"Can I get either of you something to drink before we begin?" Father Matthew asks kindly.

"No, thank you," I say.

"No, I'm good. Thank you, Father," Wes adds.

The priest lowers himself into the chair across from us and opens a folder in his lap—a dossier really. I wonder how he can have that much information on Wes and me already but the answer is clear. Gran.

"Now," The priest begins. "Let's get to know each other a bit. It says here that you, Wesley, are an FBI agent."

"Yes, Sir," he answers.

"How exciting!"

"Not really," Wes laughs. "It's mostly paperwork."

"So, nothing like the movies?" Father Matthew asks.

"No," Wes says although we both know the last year has seemed like one thriller after another.

"And you, Claire," he turns to me.

"Yes?"

"You are a detective with the George Washington Township PD."

"Yes," I answer.

"Well, is that exciting?" he asks me.

"It can be," I hedge. Wes snorts pushing the worry I had spun up all afternoon out of the way and into a full blown mad. "It's mostly tedious."

"Sure, it is," Wes mumbles.

"And do you find it fulfilling?" he asks me.

"I do," I sigh.

"You don't anymore?"

"I do . . . at least I did. Today, I'm just tired." And I am. There is a world weariness on my shoulders knowing that Wes is so angry with me all because he doesn't understand. I feel frustrated—trapped really—in an outcome that's not only not of my choosing, but I also can't fix it.

"Ha!" Wes laughs sarcastically. "Claire will always find her job fulfilling."

"That's not true," I tell him.

"Isn't it, though?" Wes asks.

"No, it's not," I tell him. "If you had stopped for one minute today to listen to me, or even stuck around this morning, you would know that you are wrong right now."

"So, you're not on the Adams case anymore?" he asks. Wes leans back in his chair crossing his arms over his chest as if he hasn't a care in the world. It's a trap and we both know it. I narrow my eyes on him.

"Well . . ." I hedge.

"So, you are still on the case?" he questions me with that formidable look on his face and his whole-body language that he shows suspects that he does not believe and that kills.

"Yes," I admit to him feeling like I'm boxed into a corner and I can't find my way out. This is like an out of body experience. A nightmare.

"Do you not want Claire on this case?" Father Matthew asks.

"Claire knows how I feel," Wes says as he crosses his arms over his chest.

"And how does Wes feel, Claire?" Father Matthew

asks me.

"He wants me off the case," I admit.

"But you're still on the case knowing how your partner feels about the situation?"

"Yes," I sigh. "But it's not what you think."

"Yeah, right," Wes barks.

"It's true!" I shout. "I talked to Lee last night. I asked him to take me off the Adams case."

"Then why are you still working it?" Wes asks, his voice deadly quiet. Wes might bellow and yell and make a lot of noise, but the truth is, he's most dangerous when he's quiet.

"Because the department is overwhelmed right now. Lee won't let me off the case," I explain knowing that after all we have been through, if I didn't know it was true, it would sound like bullshit to my own ears.

"Bullshit!" Wes thunders.

"It's true! He told me this morning that I could work the case and take my orders with a smile on my fucking face or I could turn in my badge." The pain in my voice at my brother's betrayal is there for anyone to hear if they are listening.

"Lee would want you off this case more than anyone. Even me."

"You would think that, but he doesn't, for whatever reason." I feel a scowl pull at my face. I know what the asshole formerly known as my brother is up to. He wants a link to Emma through me and if he can't have her, it won't bother him if my relationship falls to shit too.

"But you know why?" Wes asks me. I shrug. "Claire."

"I don't know for sure," I sigh. "But I think he wants a link to Emma through me."

"He wouldn't sink that low over a woman," Wes says. I just raise my brow in question. "Well, maybe for this one he would. But still . . ."

"Lee and Emma?" Father Matthew asks. "Two of our new singles members?"

"Yes, exactly," I answer.

"You're lying," Wes rallies. "Lee wouldn't sabotage my relationship because he's bitter."

I let out a heavy breath but so does the priest.

"I have to admit, your relationship is a little daunting," he starts.

"You're telling me," I gripe.

"At this juncture, I think you should go home and really evaluate what you want here." I look to the priest with wide eyes.

"What do you mean?" I ask starting to panic.

"I have to say, at least on paper, you two might be the most incompatible couple I have ever met." He sighs. "I'm sorry, but I'm not sure you should be getting married."

"Oh, okay," I say feeling dejected. I was wrong. Wes not showing up was bad but not the end of the world. Even a priest knows that we don't belong together. The only problem is, I don't want anyone else. Only Wes.

"Hold up," Wes says. "We're plenty compatible as long as she isn't lying to me."

"I'm not lying," I say feeling beyond exhausted, both physically and mentally all of a sudden.

"I'm going to stay in a hotel near the office tonight.

Let me know when you decide to be honest," he says to me.

"Don't bother," I say as I stand up and head for the door to the office. "It's your house. Just give me an hour to get some stuff together." I don't have anything but some old shitty furniture there, but the apartment is still mine. I could go back there at any time. Part of me wonders if I haven't let it go yet because I always knew, even if only in the back of my mind, that this was going to happen all along.

"Claire, wait," Wes demands, but I don't. I'm so tired and disappointed and hurt. It really hurts that he's so quick to believe I lied to him to stay on the case.

I pull open the door with Wes on my heels. It takes only a second to realize that the entire singles group heard everything. Lee looks uncomfortable as he swallows hard.

"Lee? Brother, is it true?" Wes asks.

A disgusted look flashes across Emma's face while Anna just looks so very sad. I catch Lee's quick nod before pushing my out of the church and through the parking lot to my SUV. When I climb inside and start the engine my hands shake.

But it's not until I'm driving away that I let the tears fall.

chapter 18

so fucking sorry

I DON'T RUSH HOME or drive like a crazy person. I know what waits for me and that's okay. It's not okay, but I'm not going to die on the turnpike because I got my feelings hurt. But now I just want to get in there, get my shit and get gone before I lose it. I'm walking a knife's edge of emotions right now.

I pull into the driveway and put it in park before climbing out.

My whole body starts to shake, little by little, rolling over me like a wave cresting in the ocean, as I make my way up the front walk, as I unlock the front door and walk through the house. I stop in the kitchen and grab the bottle of bourbon that I keep for very special occasions as these. I don't open it, just carry it with me to stick in my bag. I'll drink it later when I'm back in my shit hole apartment.

I walk up the stairs and into the bedroom setting the bottle on top of the dresser. By the time I walk through the bedroom and see the bed where we had slept together for the last time with the sheets still rumpled.

I didn't have it in me to make the bed this morning after I woke up and knew that Wes was gone.

I have to cover my mouth with my hand to choke back a sob. The pain burns through my chest and a sweat breaks out all over my body. I feel sick to my stomach. I feel sick in my heart.

I take a deep, steadying breath. It doesn't help so I walk into the closet and grab my duffle bag off of a shelf. I toss it on the bed and open it before walking back into the closet. I let my tears flow freely, it's better to get them out than keep them in, but I only have an hour so I have to keep packing.

I grab a handful of t-shirts and underwear. I'll come back for a couple pairs of jeans and socks in a minute. I can only carry so much in my arms. I walk out of the closet and drop them in my bag.

"So that's it?" Wes asks from behind me making me jump because I didn't hear him come in. "You're just going to leave me?"

I turn to look at him, his face is a little bruised and his knuckles are bleeding. He's leaning against the dresser and drinking my bourbon straight from the bottle.

"You're the one who was going to sleep in a hotel," I answer. "This is your house. It always has been, and it always will be. I even always knew I would have to find a new place when you eventually moved on."

"And you think that's what I want?" he repeats my words back to me before taking another swig from the bottle. I can't read the look on his face to know what he's asking. "To move on?"

At this point I'm not even sure what he's asking. Wes was so angry that he wanted to sleep in a hotel instead of with me. That thought still burns. But now he's here and I'm not sure where we stand. I hate feeling like I am on uneven footing, like I might slip and fall at any moment.

"I'm not real sure of anything right now, Wes," I admit hearing my own voice thick with emotion.

"I'm sorry, Claire," Wes says as he sets down the bottle and moves closer to me. "I'm so fucking sorry."

"It's okay," I say softly as he pulls me into his arms. His lips are just inches away from mine, he smells like bourbon and Wes. It's a heady combination.

"It's not. Don't go," he pleads. "Don't go, baby. I never want you to go. I was just so mad . . . and scared."

"I know," I say lightly touching my fingertips to his bruised cheek. "What happened here?"

"I beat the shit out of your brother in a church." He lets out a heavy sigh.

"How did that come about?" I ask.

"I realized that he's being a dick because he put his life in the crapper and now he is taking it out on us," Wes sighs running a hand through his hair. "And I realized I should have believed you when I didn't. At the very least, I should have listened, and I got pissed when I looked at his face and realized the truth."

"Wow," I say for lack of anything better.

"I'm not one hundred percent sure we're going to be allowed back there. I'm also not one hundred per-cent sure I give a rat's ass either." I laugh, I can't help it. A lightness rolls over him slowly, like a dawn rising.

"He probably deserved it." I shrug.

"He did. Don't go, baby." He pulls me in tighter resting his forehead on mine.

"Okay," I say before his mouth crashes down on mine.

Wes does not conquer or plunder, he praises me with his mouth like a requiem before breaking away to sweep my bag and clothes onto the floor. The wildness of his actions takes my breath away. When he turns back to me and slowly peels my shirt from my body there's a tenderness in his eyes that I have never seen before. An unsure longing and a vulnerability brought out by the tension of the moment and the bourbon.

My bra goes next, Wes quickly unsnaps it and tosses it to the floor on top of my t-shirt. He cups my breasts in his hands tenderly before swiping his thumbs across my nipples and I arch my back into him. I have to hold onto his belt for balance. My fingertips sliding just underneath the waistband of his slacks to touch his hot skin where it lays hidden from view.

I slide my hands up underneath his shirt and rake my nails lightly down his abs before sliding them out and moving them to the placquet of buttons down the front. When each one is undone, I push the fabric from his shoulders and gasp at the deep purple bruise on his ribs. Tenderly, I touch the tip of my index finger to his still rapidly purpling bruise.

"Lee isn't one to take a beating lying down." He shrugs. "He got in a good punch or two. Now, where were we?" he asks as he grabs me by my ass and lifts me up, his hard length pressing against my center.

I have to grab hold of his shoulders to keep from falling when he bites down where my shoulder and neck meet, sucking the skin deeply. He soothes the hurt with his tongue and a tremor wracks my body. Wes is, after all, fantastic with his tongue.

And then I'm flying through the air, letting out an undignified squeak as I land in surprise. Not really flying, but falling quickly as Wes tossed me backwards onto the bed. I lay there and just watch without shame or trying to hide my interest at all as he undoes the buckle on his belt letting it hit the carpeted floor with a muted clank. He undoes the clasp and pulls down the zipper on his pants pushing them down with his boxer briefs. His hard cock springs free and I want it. I want him.

"I need you, Claire," he says as he pops the button on my jeans and pulls down the zipper.

"You have me, Wes," I breathe.

He pulls my jeans and panties down my legs before tossing them to the floor and he pushes my legs wide settling in between them, tracing a finger through my slit.

"Always so wet for me," he growls. "You're perfect."

"Wes," I beg. I can't help the needy sound to my voice as he circles his fingertip around my clit.

"I don't want to be too rough with you," he says as he replaces his finger with the tip of his cock. "I can't hurt you anymore.

"You can't hurt me even if you tried, Wes. I won't break. And besides, I like you wild," I say honestly.

"You really shouldn't have said that," he tells me as he plunges all the way in.

I moan and rock my hips into his as he pumps over

and over. I scrape my nails down his back as he hits the spot deep inside me that drives me wild, scraping it over and over again.

"Don't ever leave me," he chants. "Don't ever leave."

"Never," I cry out as he thrusts harder and harder.

"You're mine, Claire," Wes growls as he moves faster and faster, more and more wild. "Say it."

"I'm yours," I say as I cling to him with my arms and legs wrapped tight around him as he moves faster and faster within my body.

"I need you, Claire," he pleads. "I need you so much."

"You have me," I say my voice high pitched and needy as he pumps his cock again and again. I'm so close that it won't take much to send me over the edge.

"I need you to get there," he says as my body clenches around him.

"Wes—" I pant, rocking against him to gain a little more friction. I just need a little . . . more.

"You're there." He thrusts hard.

"Yes," I tell Wes.

"And you'll never leave." He plunges in again.

"No, Never," I promise.

"You're mine." He moves faster and faster becoming more frantic as we get closer to the edge.

"Yes. Yes." I tuck my head into his shoulder needing as much of my skin touching his as possible.

"Only mine."

"Yes." And then I'm soaring, crying out his name, "Wes!" He plunges in one more time coming with me. We lay there, still clinging to each other. We've come too close to losing each other—what we have between us in one way or another—to not be moved by the moment. I feel the tears burn in my nose and behind my eyes.

"Why the tears?" he asks me softly as he wipes one away with the very tip of his index finger. "I hate to see you cry."

"I just love you so much," I whisper into the night.

I revel in the heavy feeling of his body pressing into me. And then he pulls out and rolls, taking me with him.

"I thought I had lost you tonight," he whispers into my hair.

"Me too," I tell him honestly. "It didn't feel very much like you wanted to have me."

"I'm so sorry," he says brushing my hair back from my face. "I'm so fucking sorry."

I lift his bruised and bloodied hand to my mouth and kiss just above his torn flesh. "Me too."

"I'm sorry I didn't believe you. It'll never happen again. I swear it on my life," he vows.

"Okay," I say softly not wanting to think about a time when he might have to cash in that vow. "I believe you."

"I believe you too," he says to me softly.

"I chose you, Wes," I tell him looking into his eyes so that he can see the truth lying there laid bare for all to see. "I'm going to always choose you from now on."

"I know," he says softly into the night. "And I'm going to do my best every day for the rest of my life to make sure that you never regret that."

"I know you will," I say with a mischievous twinkle in my eye.

"Oh yeah? How so?"

"You can start now," I say as I climb over him, straddling his hips. "I have a few ideas." And then I sink down over his hard cock.

Wes glides his hands up my sides, cupping a breast in each hand. I place my hands over his and squeeze showing him what I want as I start to move. I lean back letting his pull on my breast keep me balanced as I rise up and slide down his cock over and over again. His hips rise to meet mine each time making that slide down just a little bit sharper. Providing that little bit of bite that we both need.

"Wes," I pant. It's coming over me so fast that I'm helpless to stop it or slow it down.

"Yes," he growls as he thrusts his hips up again. "I want it, Claire."

"Yes, yes, yes," I chant as I rise up on my knees and drop down again and again. He moves his hands to my hips pulling me sharply down onto his cock harder and harder.

"Give it to me." And then I lean forward grabbing onto his shoulder for support as I come. Wes wraps his arms tight around me and shouts his release as he follows me over the edge.

And that is how I fell asleep, wrapped safely in Wes's arms, sprawled across his body. Sometime in the night he turned, curling his body around mine, protecting me from the storm, and it was the best night's sleep I ever had.

chapter 19

I WAKE THE NEXT morning with the early morning sun streaming through the bedroom window curtains. I look over and see Wes, his face is softer in sleep, and I can't help but think that he might need a little TLC after the emotional run we took last night

I slip below the blankets and slither down his body. I settle myself on my side, eye level with the neediest part of his body. I'm going to show him how I feel with my hands and mouth.

I take his firming cock in my hand and stroke him in my fist while I place soft kisses on Wes's upper thighs. He groans in his sleep when I swipe my tongue over the very tip of him making me smile.

He tips his hips towards what he wants, and I can't help but to give it to him. I take him deep into my mouth, slowly sliding down the length of him until I can't take anymore, before pulling back and swirling my tongue around the tip again. Letting the saliva pool in my mouth, I take him deep into my mouth again and again before a large, rough hand tangles in my hair.

"Claire—" he says, his voice rough with early mornings and steamy sex. "Baby, yeah—"

I grip his length in my fist and stroke while I swirl just the very tip of him in my mouth teasing him. Wes growls a warning but I'm enjoying playing with him. When he tightens his hands on the strands of my hair and pulls, holding my head still so that he can pump his hips ever so slightly.

I take pity on him and relax, I suck him hard as he thrusts in and out of my mouth ever so slightly. Wes flexes his fingers and I feel my core tighten and become slick. I slide my hand down my belly and trace my pussy with my fingers. I'm not close, but I am turned on.

I feel him swell in my mouth and I know that Wes is almost there. I glide my hand back up my body to scratch at his thighs while I pull him deep into my mouth, feeling the end of his cock hit the back of my throat. I swallow and feel Wes push deeper down my throat,

"Claire, baby—" he chants. "I'm-I'm . . ." And I know that he's there, so I push even farther towards the back of my throat and swallow him down. I hear Wes shouts as he floods my mouth and then I swallow down every last drop.

I let him slip from my mouth with a pop and Wes uses his grip on my hair to guide me back up his body so that we're pressed chest to breast. I get only a slight glimpse of the wild look in his hazel brown eyes before he crashes his mouth down on mine, which opens underneath his letting him lick inside.

After that, Wes throws back the covers and slaps me on the ass—hard—before jumping out of the bed and hauling me out with him. I let out a little *eek!*

Wes hauls me into the shower, naked as the day I was born and turns on the water. Cool water sprays all over us and he laughs when I jump before pinning me to the wall with his hands on either side of my head, pressing against the tile, and putting his mouth on me. I open my mouth to touch my tongue to his.

As the water heats up and the steam begins to rise, Wes kisses and licks his way down my body until his is kneeling before me. He raises my leg over his shoulder with a calloused palm before repeating the process with my other leg. My back is flat against the cool tile and I about come out of my skin the second his tongue touches my center. He spears my pussy with his tongue over and over before sucking my clit deeply and grab his hair in my hands, holding him to me.

I rock against his face, digging the heels of my feet into his back as he rolls his tongue over my clit and I scream out his name.

One by one, Wes pries my fingers from his hair and then places light kisses on each of them. He gazes into my eyes and the heat that simmers there has me wanting him all over again. Wes lowers my shaky legs to the ground before standing up. His hard cock raps its way up my body letting me know that he wants me too.

"Wes," I breathe before he touches his lips to mine. He doesn't remove them, but he does keep them just over mine, not quite touching, as he raises one leg to wrap around his hip.

I feel the tip of his cock line up with my center

before Wes pushes deep inside. I have to hold on to Wes's shoulders when he really starts to move. I love the feel of the muscles in his back and shoulders as he works my body against the wall. I feel the flex and play of them in his ass under my leg. Wes's body is truly a work of art and I am more than willing to devote my life to the study if its beauty.

I stretch up, up, up onto my tip toes and arch my back against the tile trying to reach, to angle for Wes to hit the perfect spot, and he does. He leans forward and places little love bites all over my breast before taking my nipple into his mouth and sucking deep as he powers his hips into mine. When he scrapes his teeth over the pink tip I come. He lets my nipple go with a pop and pushes up, straightening his spine to tower over me as I cling to him. Wes pumps his hips once . . . twice . . . a third time and then he buries face in my neck and comes growling out my name.

And that in how Wes showed me just how *he* felt in the shower.

" 'Heal me, O God, and I shall be healed; save me and I shall be saved: for you are my praise,' " I tell him. "I'm saving you."

"Don't do this."

"I have to do this," I tell him. "You have been poisoned by lust and adultery. I'm doing you a favor."

"Is this because I cheated on Amy?" he asks grog-

gily as he pulls on his bindings. As if that could do anything.

"No, but I will add that you your list of transgressions when I pray for you," I reassure him. "This will be over quickly."

"But why?"

"Because you tasted of the flesh."

"What?" he asks but I am already raising the knife up above my head. I bring it down quickly, plunging it into his heart. A bloody cough rattles—the sound of death—but I slide the blade out and thrust it back into his flesh the way he slid his manhood into an impure woman, over and over again.

I'm sweating and winded by the time I pull my knife free one last time. But the sacrifice is worth it. I reassure myself that I am doing the Lord's work and then I slip the sharp tip just below his skin and carve an A just like before.

I spend the rest of the day chasing down dead ends and no leads on the Adams case. By all accounts and purposes, Kerrigan Adams was the perfect employee and daughter. She was even a regular church go-er. I can't find anything to link Kerrigan Adams to her killer.

And that scares me most of all because if she was chosen at random, that means Wes was right, there could be more.

When my cell phone rings at noon, I snatch it up

off of my desk like a drowning man would a lifeline.

"Goodnite," I answer without looking to see who was calling.

"Hey, it's me," Anna answers. "Lunch?"

"Yes!" I shout a little too loudly and notice heads turn in my direction.

"Meet me at the new Chinese place in thirty. Emma is coming too."

"I'll see you then," I say before she disconnects.

The new Chinese place is halfway in between Anna's office and the station. We've been itching to try it but just haven't had the time. That and Chinese food, no matter how much you love it, loses its appeal once it has been used to poison you. But that was ages ago so I'm going to allow myself to be excited.

I log off my computer, leaving it open in a police station is a mistake you only make once, and stand up. I pull my keys out of my desk drawer and lock everything up before heading down the hallway to the door that leads to the back-parking lot.

I spare Lee's firmly closed office door a quick glance before shaking my head and pressing through the glass door. I climb in my SUV and head towards the main part of town. As I stop at a red light, I wonder if there will be a break in Kerrigan's case or if I am just chasing a ghost. I hate unsolved cases but after a while, I'm going to have to move on to the next case. I wish Lee wasn't being such a bonehead and would let me turn it over to someone else, someone with a fresh set of eyes who might see things more clearly than I do and connect the dots that I'm missing.

I pull into the parking lot and hop down from my

vehicle. A bell on a red string tinkles overhead as I push the door open. I see Emma and Anna sitting in a booth towards the back of the restaurant when they wave to me and I slide in next to Anna.

"So . . ." Anna hedges.

"We ordered a round of egg drop soup and those crunchy things that are terrible for you but you love so much for the table," Emma blurts out clearly uncomfortable.

"Last night was intense," I say breaking the tension of the table.

"It was," Anna adds.

"What happened when Wes got home?" Anna asks me.

"We talked it out," I tell them.

"Is everything okay?" Emma asks.

"It's not perfect, but we're okay," I answer.

The waiter comes and we all order our lunches. We munch on soup and crunchy things for a while before I ask, "Did Wes really beat the shit out of Lee?"

"Oh yeah," Emma says as Anna says a decided, "yes," while biting her lip.

I wince. "Is he okay?"

"Yeah," Emma says nonchalantly as our meals are served, "I took Benedict Arnold home." At that it was Anna's turn to wince.

"So, wedding planning as scheduled?" Anna presses on.

"Yes."

"Are you going back to marriage classes?" she asks.

"I'm pretty sure we failed." I sigh. "Father Matthew said we were the most incompatible couple that he has ever met." At that Emma barks out a laugh.

"I'm sure it's not that bad," Anna says biting her lip again.

"It is," I reassure her on a smile. "I don't think I wanted to get married there anyway."

"I always thought I wanted to get married on the beach," Anna says in an uncharacteristically wistful way.

"That might be nice." I smile at her.

I can't help but feel like she is on a precipice, she's at a turning point in her life and I'm afraid of what she might do when everything is said and done with Lee. After we eat our lunch and pay our tab, Anna excuses herself to go back to her office. As we watch her walk away, Emma turns to me and I realize the dynamics of their little love triangle are even more dire than I had thought.

"Should I be worried?" I ask her.

"I've got it under control," she says shaking her head.

"Anything I need to know?"

"I slept with him," she admits to me. "Lee."

"I know."

"No, I slept with him again last night. I just can't seem to stay away even though I know that I should."

"Do you have feelings for him?" I ask softly.

"How could I hurt her like that? She's everything that's right and I'm everything that's wrong."

"I don't think Lee feels that way."

"When it started, I didn't know that she was in love with him," she explains.

"I know," I tell her softly.

"But now I love him too and I can't have him."

"Are you sure about that?" I ask.

"Yes," she says firmly.

"I'm sorry," I say, and I mean it. More than anything I want them to be able to be happy with whatever resolution comes about.

"Not any sorrier that I am." The ringing of my phone interrupts the line of conversation. "Saved by the bell," she mumbles.

"Goodnite," I answer.

"Detective Goodnite, this is dispatch."

"Go ahead dispatch," I respond.

"We have reports of a male body found, cause of death appears to be similar to the case you are currently working," he informs me.

"Fuck!" I bite out. "Where?"

"Behind the deli on Third and Third."

"I'm on my way."

"Everything alright?" Emma asks.

"Not even a little bit," I sigh running my hand over my forehead where no doubt a tension headache is forming. "Better come with me. There's another body and cause of death appears similar to Kerrigan Adams."

"Well, then let's go."

chapter 20

not sure

"**O**H SHIT," EMMA SAYS as we take in the scene.

Emma who is usually unflappable—especially at a crime scene—seems a bit rattled.

"What's up?" I ask.

"I know him," she whispers under her breath.

"I'm so sorry," I tell her honestly. "Where do you know him from?"

"The church singles group," she says looking around. The concerned look on her face tells me she's hoping no one heard her until we figure out how to proceed from here.

"Shit," I mumble. I knew he looked familiar, but I didn't know him.

"Yeah," she says back.

"But you didn't really know him? Or know him from before—outside the group did you?" I ask feeling extra hopeful. I can't afford to lose Emma on this case. She's the best in the dead people business and if I have to work another serial killer case I'm going to need her.

"Can you handle this, or do we need to have someone else over see it?" I continue.

"I've got it," she reassures me.

"I need to call Wes," I tell her as I come up with a pretty decent plan on the fly. "If I can't turn it over to another detective, I'll pass it on to the feds."

"Lee is going to be so fucking pissed," she tells me.

"Then you'll just have to kiss his feel bads better." I wink to soften the blow of her addiction to her crappy hook-ups with my idiot brother.

"I am not your personal whore!" she shouts to me as she's walking over to the crime scene tech van causing everyone to turn and stare.

Emma is my wild card, no holds barred, crazy chick friend who will say whatever she feels like and unapologetically be herself. I love that. I also never know what's going to pop out of her mouth either. I am unapologetically who I am so I can relate—*sort of*—but Emma is bat shit crazy with a heart of gold. Why else would she be having such a tough time with this unfortunate love triangle? She can't stand the fact that she is part of what is hurting Anna and it's tearing her up.

"That's what you think!" I shout back to the music of her laughter.

I pull my phone out of my back pocket and dial a number that hasn't changed in twenty years. I spent plenty avoiding it, not calling the number, but when the rich voice sounds on the other end, I know I made the right choice.

"*Hey, baby*," he says, and I can hear the smile in his

voice. *"What's up?"*

"Oh . . . not much," I hedge.

"Are you having a good day?" he asks.

"I'm having a day," I say before pressing on. "Hey, are you busy right now?"

"I have fifty-six field agents to oversee and one hundred who work in the office, I'm always busy, baby, but for you I'll make time."

"Sure, we'll go with that," I say nervously. Shit, I hate being nervous. I am a fucking grown up. I am never nervous. I know exactly who I am and I own it. This is not a situation of my own making. I am just doing what I can to make the best of it.

"What's up?" he asks this time sounding more alert than before. So here goes nothing . . .

"I have another body," I tell him point blank.

"And?" I can hear in his voice that he doesn't understand what I'm saying. Wes isn't understanding *what kind of body* it is that I have on my hands.

"Second verse same as the first?" I crack.

"This isn't a joke, Claire."

"I know that," I snap.

"Then why are you calling me?" He sighs. It's that tone of voice Wes uses when he's more than frustrated. I can see him running his hands through his hair in my mind.

"I would like to formally hand this case over to the FBI." After a very pregnant pause I say, "I'm serious. If this is another repeater you take it. It's not worth risking us for it."

"Lee is going to have your ass for this," he tells me, but it's something I already know. I shrug even though

he can't see it.

"Yeah well, he's all bark and no bite these days," I lie.

"*Honey, he could take your badge for this*," he says softly. Now it's my turn to sigh because Wes is right. Lee has been looking for years for a way to fire me or get me to quit and here I am, handing him one on a silver platter.

"Well, then maybe I'll just go out on my own and be the best PI New Jersey has ever seen, like those books Gran reads about that Stephanie girl. What's that author's name? Janet Something, I think."

"Claire—"

"Wes, honey, let's just cross that bridge when we get there," I say.

"*Okay, baby,*" he says softly. "*Tell me where you are.*"

"Behind the deli on Third and Third."

"*I know the place. I'll be there in ten, hang tight.*"

"You know I will," I say just before he disconnects the call.

I make my way back to the scene and the officers who are monitoring the area and keeping looky-loos out. I take more than a cursory look this time. A man, probably early forties, with sandy brown hair and a lean build. He's leaning back against the exterior wall of the deli with his legs out in front of him and his ankles crossed casually. If it wasn't for the gruesome stab wounds all over his torso, I would think he was just resting.

"We need to talk," Emma says in a low voice when she reaches my side.

"We do," I confirm.

"There's an A," she says, her voice low, filled with worry and secrets.

"Shit. What else?"

"Like I said before," she says pausing to take a deep breath. "He was there last night. His name is Dennis and he's a dentist. I know because Anna and I kept calling him 'Dennis the Dentist' and now I feel like an asshole because he's dead."

"You didn't kill him, did you?" I ask looking at her sideways. "You know women with traumatic past relationships often go on to become serial killers."

"I hate you," she says as she slaps my shoulder.

"No, you don't." I wink.

"And Anna would say you're full of shit on the serial killers bit."

"Probably." I shrug.

"I'm not sure we're cut out for church groups," she says to me with mock seriousness.

"Me either." I sigh dramatically. We both take one look at each other and then laugh until we're interrupted by Lee's shouting.

"What the hell is going on here?" he barks.

"A murder investigation," I say as Emma and I turn to see not only is Lee standing behind us, but so is Wes. They both look like shit, but I get a modicum of joy out of the fact that Lee looks worse. He shouldn't have been such an asshole about this case. He could have sat us both down like adults—like the professionals we are—but he didn't and now he looks like his ass was handed to him last night, because it was.

"I see that, I mean him." He points to Wes.

"Special Agent in Charge O'Connell is here in a professional capacity," I answer Lee's question. What a fun turn of events after the last year of Lee trying to hand my cases to Wes, here he is now acting like a jerk because I am trying to do that very thing. Where's the popcorn?

"At whose request?" he snaps.

"Mine."

"You're fired!" he roars.

"Sure thing, boss." I shrug.

"You're just going to fire your sister?" Emma shouts snapping her fingers. "Just like that?"

"Yes," he says his tone neutral as he quotes her question. "'Just like that.'"

"Then you are a bigger idiot than I had originally thought," she says sadly as she walks away.

"You don't get to walk away from me, Dr. Parker," he shouts to her back.

"Watch me," Emma volleys back flipping him off over her shoulder, not ever bothering to turn around and look him in the eye. I watch the muscle in his cheek twitch and think *not my circus, not my monkeys.*

"Well, clearly you have this under control," I say patting Lee on the chest. "Since you don't need me, I'll just be heading out."

"I *might* have spoken too soon," Lee says.

"I'm sorry," I say holding up my hand to my ear. "I can't hear you due to your advancing age and all, what did you say?"

"I said I was wrong," he tells me. "And you're not fired."

"Thank you," I say softly. "So, let's turn this over

to Wes and get back to normal."

"Not so fast," he says quickly.

"What?" Wes and I both look to Lee at the same time.

"I do not agree with handing this case over to the FBI," Lee says, this time more calmly than before.

"Dude, it's clearly going to be another messy one. That's not for me right now," I tell him the truth.

"So, you're not wanting to be a detective anymore?" Lee asks me.

"That's not what I'm saying," I say trying to defend my actions.

"Then what *are* you saying?" he snaps.

"That my voice is forever changed from being nearly strangled to death a few months ago," I say after taking a deep breath. "I'm saying I'll be fine, but my next case should not be another serial killer."

"Okay, I hear you," Lee concedes.

"Thank you."

"I'll agree to an FBI collaboration between you and Wes but that's it. This case stays within the department."

"You are such an ass," I mumble under my breath and Wes busts out a deep laugh. "Well, you can be my first witness interview."

"What?" Lee asks.

"I have been informed that the victim is Dennis Boyd of last night's Singles Group," I say feeling just a little smug about knocking Lee off-kilter for even just a little bit. I bite back a smirk.

"No shit?" he asks.

"No shit," I confirm.

"Why don't we all pitch in here for awhile," Wes wades in "And then we can all go to dinner and discuss what might have happened to Mr. Boyd?"

"Sounds good to me," Lee says.

"Me too," I agree.

"Good, you can talk to Emma and Anna," Wes says.

And that's exactly what we did. We closed up the scene together—Wes, Lee, Emma and me.

I regretted having dinner as a group from the moment we sat down.

What was Wes thinking? There is no way we should have Anna and Emma at dinner with Lee. We might as well pour gasoline all over this trendy restaurant with its mood lighting and its fusion cuisine and then play with matches.

That's exactly what being here is, playing with matches. Or a fucking bomb.

"So, tell me a little about Dennis," I ask.

"He flirted with Emma a little," Anna says. Lee narrows his eyes looking less than pleased but thankfully, he stays relatively silent. *For now*.

"But he left with that girl that was all over Lee, what was her name?" Emma asks.

"Sarah Holt," Lee says.

"That's right." She snaps her fingers as she remembers. "Slutty Sarah was all over Lee and then went off with Dennis the Dentist when class let out."

"I like this jealous side of you," Lee says low for Emma but we all hear it. And thanks to the round table we all see the pain that flashes across Anna's face before she buries it deep. And by deep, I mean *deep*. But it's a serious effort that she is making, and it's not lost on any of us, most of all Emma.

"I'm not jealous, I just like pointing out your many cases of syphilis." She smiles sweetly.

"What else do you know about Dennis?" I ask trying to get this train back on track.

"He's divorced," Anna quickly adds. "No kids that I know of."

"He said he was lonely and wanted to marry again," Emma shares.

"I just bet he does," Lee grumbles.

"He left with Sarah to go get drinks. That was the last I saw of him," Anna shares.

"Thank you," I tell them all. Unfortunately, now we have nothing to talk about. Which is abundantly obvious as we're all pushing our food around on our plates.

"You have to talk to me, Emma," Lee voices his frustration, his voice low but again carrying around the table.

"No, I don't," she snaps. "And leave me alone."

"I can't, Em," he pleads. "You know why. Don't ask me to. Anything but that."

"Oh, look at the time," Anna says. "I have to get home and feed my cat," she says as she jumps up and tosses a bunch of bills on the table before rushing out the door.

"Are you fucking happy now?" Emma snaps.

"Yes! Because now at least you're fucking talking to me," Lee yells.

"Don't get used to it," she fires back tossing bills on the table and storming off.

"Fuck!" he thunders.

"You have to back off, Lee," I say.

"Claire—" Wes tries to stop me.

"You're hurting them," I push. "Can't you see that?"

"I can't, Claire," Lee pleads. "I need her."

"At whose expense? Anna's?" I question.

"Claire—" Wes tries again only to be cut off yet again as well.

"I never promised her anything," Lee explains.

"And that makes it right?" I can't help but ask.

"I don't know," Lee says softly.

"She's important to Emma, Lee," I tell him something he already knows.

"I know that," he lets out a breath in anger? In frustration? I don't know what and I don't care because this, all of this is his fucking fault. I'm so angry that I feel my face burn with it. This is absolutely ridiculous. The whole thing is driving me mad.

"Emma will never do anything to hurt her," I say softly, not letting any of that anger bubble over the surface.

"She'll get over it," Lee presses on. I can see by the look on his face that he's determined to have his way. I just can't help but feel that it's all about to blow up in our faces. I'm not sure who will survive it, if anyone.

"She's not getting over it, Lee." I say softly. "I don't see this working out for you."

"Claire—" Wes tries one more time.

"I'm in love with her," Lee says dropping his bomb one more time in my lap.

"Shit," I bite out.

I'm not sure if I thought the situation was ever going to change or if I thought he would lose interest or what. But Lee's decisions, his actions, are affecting more than just him and he is being so narrow minded that he can't seem to understand that.

"Yeah," Lee agrees.

Leave it to Wes to break the silence as he raises a hand in the air and calls out, "Check please!"

chapter 21

blood

I'M LOST IN THOUGHT.

I brood the entire car ride home from dinner. Just when I think I have my life on track everything falls to shit. For years, I fought tooth and nail for every scrap. Every case that could possibly make my career, take me to the next level. To say I was driven would be a major understatement.

And now I'm stuck on a high-profile case that I don't even want.

And why don't I want it? Because it could cost me greatly. It could cost me Wes. Because I might have been near to strangled by a deranged serial killer a couple months ago, but it was Wes who found me. It was Wes who saved my life. I might be traumatized, and it might have changed me, but that day changed him too. I can't blame him for that.

And on top of all that, my brother is being a Grade A asshole and I am powerless to stop it. He is so lost to Emma that he can't see that he's turning everyone else's life upside down in the process. And poor Anna is never going to be the same. Hell, neither is Emma. The whole thing is tearing her apart. My stomach burns as my thoughts tumble around in my brain like a load of wash in the dryer.

And on top of everything, I have another serial killer to find. Because what kind of person hacks up people and carves an initial into their bodies? A psycho. I don't even need Anna to spell that one out for me.

Because we arrived at the scene separately, we had both of our vehicles out and about, no cozy carpooling for Wes and me. Although, I think we could use the time to ourselves to think about all that has happened in the last couple of days. At least, I know I can.

I pull into the driveway beside Wes as he waits for me. He doesn't go on ahead to open the door or go on into the house, he waits for me in the driveway and walks up with me. That's the kind of thing that sticks in my mind. Wes cares for me in a way that no one ever has before. He genuinely wants to spend every minute he can with me, making up for time we had lost.

"A penny for your thoughts, babe," he says softly as he opens the front door.

"What?" I ask.

"Honey, it doesn't take a crystal ball to see that you're a million miles away."

"I'm sorry," I tell him genuinely.

"It's going to be okay, Claire," Wes reassures me.

"Are you so sure of that?" I ask. "Because I can't help but feel like nothing is ever going to be the same again." Wes wraps me up in his arms, holding me tight.

"Then let's go to bed, baby. Maybe everything will

seem better in the morning."

"Okay," I tell him.

I let Wes lead me up the stairs. I let him slowly undress me, piece by piece, before tucking me into bed. I watch with rapt attention as he strips off his fed suit, button by tiny little button. Wes has an amazing body that he obviously works hard at keeping when I'm not paying attention. I, on the other hand, nourish mine with butter and pizza. Different strokes for different folks, I guess.

"What's that look for?" he asks as he shucks his pants to the floor.

"I was just admiring your beautiful body," I tell him honestly and watch him preen at the compliment, so I can't help but poke him a bit. "It's obvious you work hard at it despite your advanced age."

"Advanced . . . advanced age!" he blusters. "I'll show you advanced age!" he shouts as he pounces on me.

I let out an undignified squeak and roll to the side trying to make a quick exit, but he grabs me by the waist and flips me to my belly. His broad palm lands hard on my ass and I yelp.

"Wes!" I complain but we both know that it's half-hearted because even I can hear the laughter in my voice.

"So, you think I'm an old man, do you?" he asks as he pulls me to my hands and knees.

"I don't think, I know that you're an old man," I say with wide eyes as positions himself behind me. "Do you know that they say that forty is the beginning of the end? I should start shopping for your convalescent home tomorrow."

"We'll just see about that," he says as he thrusts his cock deep inside me and I can't stop the moan that falls from my lips as he hits that magic spot deep inside.

"Wes," I pant as I drop down to my forearms and brace.

I know that this will be a wild ride, so I brace myself and Wes does not disappoint as he powers deep. Neither of us will last long like this and I don't care. I love Wes best when he is wild and free. After the last couple of days we both need this release, this moment away from everything else.

Here we are just Wes and Claire, the rest of the world can wait.

"I need you to get there, baby," Wes growls as he plunges deep in a hard and fast rhythm. "Touch yourself. I need you to get there."

I balance myself on my left arm and shoulders, gripping the sheet in my fist for purchase as I slide my other arm between my body and the bed down, down, down until I can feel the side of his cock where his body enters mine and it's a heady feeling to touch the very place where we join together with my fingertips grazing him as I go.

"Claire—" he warns his fingers digging into my hips and I move my own fingers to my clit and circle.

I gasp when my finger hit my heated flesh. "Yes."

"I want it," I says as he plunges in again and again and I'm helpless to do anything but to give him what he wants. As my climax washes over me I hear him call out my name as he follows me over the edge.

Wes and I fall in a sweaty, breathless pile and he

rolls us to the side, my back to his front and he curls around me pulling the blankets up over us. He buries his face in that crook between my neck and shoulder, a place he focuses on most of the time, and chuckles in my ear. His voice gravel smooth and still rough with sex, "Advanced age, my ass."

And then we both drifted off to sleep. Too bad it would prove to be a restless one and in the coming days I would look back and wish I had trusted my gut when it warned me otherwise. Nothing here is as it seems. And even though I let Wes feel like he convinced me differently, I still can't help but feel like something very bad is about to happen. If I hadn't pretended to agree, maybe things could have turned out differently. But then again, I guess we'll never know.

Run!

I'm running as fast as my little feet will take me through the woods behind my parents' house. I have to get away from the bad man. If he catches me now, I'll never get away. I have to be free.

Run! I have to run faster.

I see the blue gray light as it spills through the trees. Mommy always told me this was her favorite part of the day—looking at the sun as it comes up in the morning. I ran away late in the night when the bad man was sleeping. It was my only chance. After he broke the lock on the closet door I knew that I had a chance to get out. I wasn't trapped anymore with nothing to stop me.

I had to get home. I push the door to the outside open and take my first breath of fresh air. The air inside was dusty and gross. I didn't like the smell of it at all. But now I'm outside and free. But I have to run or else the bad man will catch me.

Free.

I'm free. That's the words in my head as the trees break and I see Wes standing at the edge of the backyard. I'm free. I'm finally free. Wes looks up and he sees me.

"I've got her!" he shouts to someone.

My heart is beating so hard in my chest and it hurts to breathe but I try to suck in as much as I can. I'm so tired but I have to keep running. I can see Wes standing on the edge of the woods looking back at me. I can tell just by looking at his face that he'll protect me. Wes always protects me. He will keep me safe. He will keep me free. Forever.

I push my feet just a little harder, I run just a little faster. I'm almost there. I'm almost free when he reaches for me and I collapse in Wes's arms. But when I look down, I'm covered in blood. There's so much blood that it's everywhere. All over my clothes and Wes's. There is blood all over the trees and it soaks the moss and dirt of the forest floor. It's clogging my lungs and I can't breathe. It's smeared across his face and matted in my hair. It's in my mouth and all over my hands.

I look up into Wes's dead eyes. I always knew the bad man would kill me I just didn't know he would get Wes too. There's a pain in my chest where my heart used to be. I know for sure that it's broken because my sweet Wes is dead and it's all my fault.

I open my mouth and scream . . .

Earthqake.

My body is being thrown about so bad that it must be an earthquake. No, it's hands on my body, shaking me. For a second, I'm still gripped in my dream and think that the bad man has me again until I hear Wes's deep voice.

"Claire, you're safe," he says as he shakes me again. "Wake up, baby. You have to wake up."

"Wes?" I ask gulping in as much air as I can and choking because my lungs still sear with panic. I blink my eyes open several times to clear the sleep and the lasting effects of my nightmare. "You're alright?"

"No, I'm not fucking alright, baby," he growls.

"What's wrong?" I ask feeling alarm trill through my body.

"Your nightmares."

For a minute I flash back to the time when I was so deep in my puppy love for Wes that I gave him my virginity at eighteen and he threw it back in my face because he had witness my having a night terror so bad he knew that he couldn't save me. I didn't know it then, but Wes had thought he was doing what was best for me by pushing me away. He had no way of knowing that I wouldn't tell anyone about my nightmares and how they torture me through all hours of the night. He had thought that my family would get me help and one day everything would be hunky dory.

Lately, he swears he'll follow me into my own person hell to pull me back out again, but I have always wondered if there would come a time that he can't handle it and now I can't help but wonder if that's the case. My heart stutters before it speeds up and my face feels hot. He must see the look of alarm cross my face because he speaks quickly.

"It's not that, baby. I'm not going anywhere," Wes reassures me. "But they're coming more often."

"I know." But I don't know. In the back of my mind, I am always wondering when Wes will leave me because he can't take it anymore.

"We have to do something about them, honey," he says softly.

"I don't know how." And it's true. If I did know how to fix them, to fix me, I would.

"You can't go on like this," Wes tells me something that I already know, and I do know. I know that I can't survive like this forever. But I also haven't been willing to really dive deep and get to the root of the problem. Anna has been after me for forever to do some deep hypnosis therapy mumbo jumbo and I have been avoiding the task for a long time. Maybe now it's time to stop running. But still, I don't really want to . . .

"You think I don't know that?" I try to push away from him but his arms close tight around me, holding me to him.

"We'll get through it."

"You're tired of it." I feel the tears sting the backs

of my eyes before the wet hits my cheeks. "I knew you would get tired of having to deal with it."

He sighs. "I'm tired of seeing you hurt, baby. I don't want to see you suffer anymore. But I'm not fucking going anywhere."

"Yeah, but for how long?" I can't help but ask. As soon as the words leave my mouth I instantly want to pull them back in.

"Forever."

"You can't mean that," I say. How can he promise me everything when so much is still hanging in the balance? "You can't say that."

"I just did."

"Wes—" I start but he interrupts me. Again.

"I'll promise you the moon and mean it because I love you. If these nightmares never stop I'll still be by your side because I love you that much. But I want you to live a life of peace and beauty because you deserve it but also because I love you and also selfishly, I want to be the one to give you that."

"Wes," I whisper this time with my heart in my throat. "I love you too."

"I know it," he says smugly. "Now, go back to sleep. Tomorrow is going to be a long day." And I did. I curled up in the safety of Wes's strong arms and went to sleep. It would be later that I would realize that I should have stayed awake and basked in the beauty of my life the way that it was because very soon, everything would change.

chapter 22

the missing piece

*B**EEP . . . BEEP . . . BEEP . . .*
I wake to the sound of Wes's alarm on the nightstand and his arms still heavy around my body. The early morning light is just starting to sift through the bedroom windows and I can't help but feel like his words from the middle of the night will ring true. It's going to be a long fucking day.

"Are you still a million miles away?" Wes asks me as he brushes my hair back from my face to behind my ear.

"Yes and no," I answer.

"What's bothering you, baby?" Wes asks me.

"Something's wrong," I pause in answering his question. "I just can't put my finger on what. It's like a bad omen or something, but something is really wrong."

"It's your brother," he guesses on a sigh.

"Maybe a little," I say and when he raises a brow questioning the veracity of my comment I continue.

"Okay that's part of it . . . a *big* part of it."

"You interfered after I told you not to and didn't like the answers you found." Wes sighs before tracing a finger down my cheek. "I knew you would be disappointed. As cheesy as it sounds I hate seeing you anything but happy. I know that it has to happen, that's life, right? But I still hate it."

"No! Yes. I don't know." I sigh. "Emma keeps hooking up with Lee behind Anna's back. Then talking shit about him in front of her face. It's so weird and twisted and stupidly reckless but that's not it."

"That's their business, baby," he says in response when really I was thinking he would say something like "That's crazy! What's gotten into those assholes?" Wes's lack of shock hits me like a sack of bricks and it dawns on me the missing piece to my puzzle.

"You knew!" I demand. "You filthy lying bastard! You knew that my brother was wrecking lives with his dick and didn't tell me so that I could try and stop it."

"Yes."

"And you didn't tell me!" I cry out in all my anger.

"No, I didn't," Wes says calmly.

"Well, why the hell not?" I demand getting all worked up over it.

"Because it's none of our business and Lee confided in me as his oldest friend," he explains calmly. "Also, because there's nothing you can do about it."

"You don't know that!" I yell. And he doesn't know for sure. Who's to say that I couldn't have talked some sense into Emma or even Lee before hearts became involved and they all got too deep in the bullshit to wade their way out? Maybe I could have stopped them all from falling in love with the wrong someone.

"I do," he says. "They have to figure this out on their own."

"But they're going to fuck it up!" I complain and Wes laughs.

"Yeah, honey, they are but so did we and look where it got us," he says squeezing his arms around me. "Now, let's go to work and fight crime like the badasses we are. Then tonight we'll pray our closest friends pull their heads out of their asses. Sound good?"

"That's probably as much as I can ask for," I sigh.

"Great!" he says smacking my ass. "Let's go." And then he throws the bedding back and knifes out of the bed taking me with him.

"It's the exact same," Emma informs me from her desk when I step out of the elevator in her dungeon—I mean basement morgue.

"It can't be," I respond.

Wes and I had showered together. Then actually took the time to have breakfast in our kitchen together since we weren't carpooling today before he kissed me goodbye in the driveway.

"I'll see you later, babe. Call me if anything comes up in the case."

"Will do, bossy man." I shot him a mock salute. Wes stops his descent into his car and narrows his eyes on me over the roof of his Fed-mobile. "What?"

Wes stalked back around to where I was standing next to my Tahoe. "Don't be cute and make me want to fuck you when I need to go to work."

"Who's being cute?" I asked. I shrugged my shoulders. "This is just me."

"I know it's you, but you are anything but just," he said as he pulled my body into his. "Everything you do is cute and everything you do makes me hard."

"I can tell," I laughed because the proof of his statement was pressing into my belly.

"Claire—" he warns just before he crushed his mouth to mine and I was lost in a swirling storm of teeth and tongues and bodies pressed tight, to heat and lust. Suddenly the predicament isn't so funny.

"Have a good day at the station, baby," Wes said before walking away from me to jump in his car and head off to work with a pretty fucking smug expression on his stupid handsome face. All while I was left standing in our driveway wondering what had just happened. I shook my head like a etch-a-sketch and then hopped in my Tahoe to head to the station.

About a nanosecond after I had pushed through the glass doors Emma called for me to head down to the morgue because she was finished with the autopsy of Dennis Boyd. Now I'm standing here with her in her creepy basement morgue wondering what wrongs I had done in my life to land two serial killer cases back to back.

"Did you hear me?" she asked.

"Yeah." I swallow past the lump in my throat. "I heard you."

"From the bump on the head to the ligature marks

on the wrists, it's all the same."

"Walk me through it one more time, now that I know that there are two of them. Tell me step by step, how they are the same," I ask as I pull my notebook out of my back pocket and snatch a pen off the top of her desk.

"You better return that when you're done!" she snaps. Our Emma is a wee bit of a Nazi when it comes to her stationary and office supplies.

"Yes, Mistress," I say on a mock bow.

"That's better." She preens in a haughty manner.

"Can we move along now?" I ask. "I would hate for Lee to figure out where we are and wander down here. He'd only get in the way." I hate to use their issues against them, but I have shit to do so I need her to focus.

"Uhh . . . yeah . . . he'd only . . . uhh, get in the way." I take one look at her splotchy face and realize what she's saying without words.

"Dude, you banged him again?"

"I can't help myself where he's concerned." She throws her arms up in the air before bringing them back down to cover her red fucking face. "I hate him, and I don't want anything to do with him. But then he crooks his finger at me and before I know it, I fall on his magical penis and come to when the orgasm settles."

"There is so much wrong with that entire statement," I stare at her with what has to be a horrified expression on my face. "I'm going to need you to refrain from using phrases like, magic penis and orgasm around me when referencing my brother. That's just gross, yo."

She sighs. "I know."

"So back to the autopsy . . ."

"Oh, right," she begins. I can see Emma mentally shake off her own personal woes. "Both victims have large contusions on their heads. I would guess that that is how they were subdued."

"That makes sense. Kerrigan Adams was a petite woman, but Dennis Boyd was fit and about six feet tall."

"Yes, exactly," she says. "They both also have abrasions on their wrists from being bound."

"There was no rope or cuffs at either crime scene," I remind her.

"Yes, but the skin doesn't lie," she says. "I did some impressions and it matches a standard jute cord you can buy just about anywhere so that was probably a wasted effort." She shrugs.

"You never know." And it's true. Even the most obscure piece of evidence or fact can be what brings the whole case together. You just never know until it's right in front of your face.

"Also, both victims were stabbed to death but the way the stab wounds bled suggests the first wound was to the heart and death would have been quick. The initial A was also carved into the skin in the chest area postmortem on both victims."

"Still gross," I say off hand.

"That it is, my friend. That it is." She's got a weird sense of humor, this one, but then again, when you work in our field and see how cruel people can be, you kind of have to have one to survive.

"Thanks, chick. I'll see you later," I say as I make

my way over to the elevator.

When the doors open back upstairs—or really, above ground—I head back to my desk and pull out every note, every stitch of paper, every piece of evidence in the case no matter how small or trivial and place it on top of my desk. Sometimes, seeing the clutter all laid out can help me spot a connection I had otherwise missed.

I need to follow up some leads on Dennis Boyd. There are too many pieces of the puzzle missing where he is concerned. I need to make some phone calls. He's not from around here so there aren't many connections to be made but still there's something.

I pick up the phone and dial the number I have for his ex-wife in Connecticut.

"Hello?" she answers.

"Adrienne Boyd?" I ask.

"It's Mrs. Michaels now, who's calling?" she asks.

"My apologies, Mrs. Michaels, I'm Detective Claire Goodnite from the George Washington Township PD, can I ask you some questions about your ex-husband?"

"Dennis?" she asks me. "I can't see why you would be asking me about Dennis but go ahead, Detective."

"Was there any tension in your marriage?" I ask.

"Not really, no," she answers. "Really, we just grew apart."

"Was your divorce amicable?"

"Why are you asking me these questions?" she asks. I can hear the frustration in her voice.

"Mrs. Michaels, Dennis Boyd is dead."

"What?" she asks. "You have to be mistaken."

"I'm not, ma'am, we have a positive ID," I inform her. "So, I'll ask again, was your divorce particularly ugly?"

"Not at all," she says quietly. "We were both mostly just over it. We were young. Dennis wasn't ready to be anyone's husband let alone mine. We're still friends today."

"Can you think of anyone who would want to harm Dennis?" I ask.

"Not at all. You can't think someone did this on purpose . . ." she lets the thought hang in the air because I can't answer it the way she wants me to before I continue with my questioning.

"Dennis Boyd was murdered, Mrs. Michaels. I'm so sorry," I say when I hear her sob over the line.

"Was there anyone or anything new in his life that you noted?" I ask.

"He was going to a new church," she answers. "Said that he was going to a singles group and that he was ready to meet someone special. My husband and I are—*were*—happy for him."

"Thank you for your time, Mrs. Michaels," I tell her. "If you think of anything else, don't hesitate to call me."

"I will," she says softly. "Just find who did this."

"I will," I promise her just before ending the call.

I place the phone in its cradle on my desk and look down at all the shit that I have accumulated one more time. Kerrigan Adams and Dennis Boyd. Their lives shouldn't have anything in common with one another and yet they do. It seems so simple that I can't believe I didn't see it sooner.

"That can't be it," I say to myself. "It can't be that simple."

But it is.

It's a tiny little detail, one that seems so silly that there is no way that could be the connection. I scan everything again three more times just to be sure. And again, there it is. I can't believe we missed this.

I pick up the phone and dial the extension for Wes's desk. If he's not in the office I'll track his ass down because this is the break we have been looking for. He picks up on the third ring.

"Special Agent O'Connell," he answers.

"Well, aren't you all fancy and shit," I droll.

"Hello to you too, Darling," he laughs. "Is there a reason your calling me at work or was it just to harass me?"

"Harassing you is a valid reason particularly because you have a nice ass," I tell him forcing my voice to sound as serious as possible even though I can barely get through the words and have to bite down on my lip to keep from laughing. I'm pretty sure Wes can tell too. Silly bastard.

"Despite my advanced age?"

"Yes, exactly." I'm nodding my head, but he can't see me. "But alas, there is a reason."

"And what pray tell, would that be?" he asks me.

"Tragically, we have to go back to marriage classes tonight." I let out a heavy sigh.

"I'm glad we're over our last drama and all," he says after a very pregnant pause. "But I thought we agreed that wasn't for us?"

"Oh, it's not," I reply. "But I was looking at the

case notes for Dennis Boyd's murder and comparing them to those of the Kerrigan Adams case. You'll never guess what I found."

"And what exactly would that be?"

"That our two victims were not only parishioners of the very church we attended marriage classes at, but they were both members of the very same singles group that our dearest friends just recently joined." I can't help sounding smug, but I do. I love that I'm the one that cracked this case wide open. I can just feel it in my bones. This is the missing piece to the puzzle.

"You're kidding," he says with all seriousness, the playfulness of earlier is long gone.

"I wish I were," I tell Wes. "Someone is killing off church singles and we're going to find out why."

"Well, I guess I don't have to worry about you getting caught in the crosshairs this time," he mumbles.

"And why is that?" I ask.

"Because you're not fucking single and you're never going to be single again," he says with finality.

"There *is* another bright side to this," I purr. "We get to send Lee back to the singles group."

"That's mean," he laughs. *"But I won't say the fucker doesn't deserve it."*

"Agreed," I say with an extra sweet tone of voice.

"You know? You're scary when you plot against family members," he tells me.

"Why thank you, Wes, that's the sweetest thing you've ever said to me."

I spend the rest of the work day making phone inquiries to try and prove my theory. Every person I have talked to so far has told me what good people they thought both Dennis and Kerrigan were—*good, church going, people*.

As it turns out both victims had been looking for love in all the *right* places before their untimely deaths this week. Which makes me wonder what's really going on here? Not to mention, both were active members of Father Matthew's very successful singles group. So when the clock strikes five o'clock, I jump in my Tahoe and head out to our favorite family church for marriage classes.

Hopefully, after the other day, they will still take Wes and me.

I'm running a little behind schedule, so I take the first available spot in the parking lot and jump out, palming my keys as I go. When I make it to the steps of the church just before the doors open for the evening Lee, Emma, and Anna are all standing there with their arms crossed over their chests staring daggers at me. Wes, on the other hand, is grinning from ear to ear like a loon and is clearly enjoying himself.

"So glad I made it in time," I say running up the steps.

"I hate you," Emma snaps.

"Yeah, what she said," Anna adds glaring at me.

I choke back a laugh, unsuccessfully I might add, when their eyes narrow on me. "This is going to be fun."

"I'm not sure I care for your definition of fun, sister dear," Lee drolls.

"Then you should have handed the Adams case off to someone else," I reply.

"Yeah, someone less sadistic than a Goodnite," Emma gripes.

"Yeah . . ." I agree wistfully.

"Good evening ladies and gentlemen," Father Matthew says as he pulls open the massive front doors of the church. Then as he takes in Wes and me, "Well, I have to admit that I am surprised to see you two here tonight."

"We're so happy to be here," I say in my best impression of a happy soon-to-be-misses.

"I take it you settled your disagreement?" he asks on a raised brow.

"Of course," I answer.

"Well, then, welcome back," he says as he waves us in.

"Thank you, Father," Wes says buttering him up.

"Father Thomas will fill in for me with the single group again tonight." A collective groan goes up around the room.

"Did I miss something?" Wes asks.

"Father Thomas can be a bit . . . *serious* from time to time," Father Matthew explains.

"I thought he was the hip, young guy everyone was all excited about?" I ask.

"He is. He's just very passionate about certain things and shall we say . . . *long winded*."

"Oh, okay." I laugh.

"Well, shall we head into the office?" Father Matthew asks.

"Sure thing," Wes says and we all head down the

short hall.

He motions for us to sit in the chairs again and we do. This time Wes keeps a hold of me placing our linked hands in his lap. The priest looks taken aback by this show of tenderness and intimacy.

"So, you resolved your tiff, did you now?" he asks.

"Yes," I answer.

"It was just a misunderstanding," Wes answers.

"So, you chose your intended over your career? That's not very modern of you," he muses.

"It's not, but I also had the choice taken away from me." I shrug my shoulder.

"So, you're still working the case?" he asks me.

"Yes," I answer him honestly not willing to expound on the subject.

"And how does that make you feel, Wesley?" Father Matthew asks him.

"Not too bad," he answers.

"What brought about the change of heart? You were pretty upset about it the other day." Father Matthew is trying to point out that we haven't really solved anything, but he doesn't know that Wes and I have talked everything out and are excited to move forward with our marriage. He also doesn't know that we're excited to catch a killer too. We just have to figure out who it is first.

"Well, for one, I understand that Claire was put in a tight spot, and two, we're working together now," Wes answers honestly.

"You're both working the investigation now?" he asks, and I can't help but wonder about his sudden interest in policing or if it has anything to do with the murders of two of his parishioners.

"Yes, we're collaborating on this case," Wes repeats.

"You know what they say?" I ask casually. "Two heads are better than one!"

chapter 23

i really hate serial killers

I'M FEELING MORE CONFUSED than ever when we walk out of the office with Father Matthew. But I stumble over a step when I walk into the main room and see the singles group also breaking up for the evening. Anna looks sick and Emma look absolutely furious. My brother, Lee, on the other hand is surrounded by a gaggle of women that I have never seen before.

"Oh shit," Wes mumbles when he comes up behind me.

"Looks that way," I reply.

"Why is he so stupid?" Wes asks me.

"I'm pretty sure they dropped him on his head a bunch as a baby," I explain.

"Well, I'm duty bound as his best friend to go bail his ass out of a sling. Care to come help?"

"No, thank you," I say sweetly. "I prefer to watch his impending doom from afar."

"Thank you so much for your compassion. It's astounding," Wes kisses me on the cheek. He laughs as he walks over to Lee.

"A bunch of us are going to that new bistro over on Cicada. I'd love it if you joined us," a petite brunette purrs as she leans into Lee's arm.

"What do you know," he answers. "My friends and I were going to dinner too. Maybe we'll see you there."

"That would be great," she says before trotting off.

I walk over to my friends eyeing the warily as I go.

"I'm never coming back here again," Emma declares upon my arrival.

"Okay," I say.

"I think it would be best if I did not come back either," Anna shares.

"Yeah, we thought it would be fun, kind of a good joke while you and Wes had your classes . . ." Emma adds before looking over at Lee and his harem. "But it's not funny anymore."

"Let's just go to dinner and talk about what you guys saw tonight. Then we'll never talk about this moment again," I plead

"Agreed," they both say at the same time.

"Ready to go, ladies?" Wes asks when he and Lee walk up to our little parlay.

"Yep, dinner," Emma says looking anywhere but at Lee's face.

"I'm thinking I'd like to try that new bistro over on Cicada," Lee says.

"Brother—" Wes warns under his breath, but I can hear it.

"I hear good things about it," Anna says.

"You're playing with fire, Lee," I warn.

"Maybe that's a good thing," he says.

"Or maybe you'll get burned."

" 'It is God's will that you should be sanctified: that you should avoid sexual immorality; that each of you should learn to control your own body in a way that is holy and honorable, Or learn to live with your own wife; or learn to acquire a wife.' I told you but you did not listen. You never listen."

But she doesn't listen. This one lusts for a husband of her own so badly that she doesn't care where he comes from. She is free with her touches and flirts unashamed! She is so unclean I have to purge her. She will understand when it is all over.

"Don't," she begs just like the common whore that she is. "Please don't do this. I won't tell anyone, I swear it."

"I know you won't tell anyone because you will be dead," I inform her. "Are you ready to meet your maker?"

"No," she says as she pulls on her bindings, but it is too late.

I pull the knife from its sheath and grip the hilt firmly in both hands high over my head. I bring the blade down swiftly plunging it into her wicked heart. I repeat the process over and over again, pulling the knife from her warm skin only to plunge it in again the way she lusts for a man's body to enter hers again and again. It is that sin that she must atone for and I am helping her. For I do the Lord's work.

I pull the blade free one more time hating every second that I have to hurry this time for fear of being discovered too soon. I dip the pointed tip into the flesh of her chest that she chose to expose with her wanton ways and carve an A for adulterer.

I slide the blade back into its sheath hidden in my clothing and with one look back at her I see that she is at peace and I know that she is with our Lord answering for her sins of the flesh.

And then I walk to the sink and wash my hands carefully letting all of the blood run free down the drain and then I dry my hands carefully on a paper towel before walking out the door and never looking back.

Regardless of whether or not it was a good idea, we all pile in our separate cars and head to the new little bistro over on Cicada. The room is dimly light with a darwood bar and cozy little tables to provide an intimate atmosphere. I can see why the singles would want to meet here to take their conversations to a more personal level.

When I walk in Lee is at the bar with the brunette and Emma is in a state. I'm kind of afraid. Judging by the look on her face that she might just set the whole building on fire. If I'm crazy she's crazier. Anna was always our voice of reason and calming influence but even she looks like she could commit murder at this particular junction. I only hope Lee is ready to reap what he sows.

When he sees me he leaves the brunette and walks over to us with a beer in his hand. The hostess takes us all to a dark booth in the back where things deteriorate further. Anna takes one look at the tight seating and pretends to take a call from a patient and leaves.

"You don't need me here anyways," she says sadly when I walk her out.

"Of course we do. Please stay," I plead but we both know that it's only a recipe for disaster. I hate Lee for breaking up our group of five.

"Nah, I don't really fit in anyways. I never did." She shrugs. I'll talk to you later."

I walk back into the bar to find that things haven't gotten any better. Lee is still an asshole and Emma is still pretending to hate him. I honestly don't know how much more of this bullshit I can take before I lose it completely. Something has to give and soon.

"I hate you more and more," I hear Emma say when I get back to the table where Lee has her wedged against the wall in the far side of the booth.

"But you love my cock, baby," he responds.

"Thank Christ you're back," Wes shouts when he sees me. "I can't take more of the *Days of Our Lives* shit happening over here." Then he downs a large portion of his beer. Yikes! It looks like I missed a lot.

"Neither can I," Emma snaps.

"How about we talk about what happened during the singles group tonight," I press. "Anything interesting happen?"

"Father Thomas preached the entire time about sins of the flesh and fornication," Lee says. "He seems pretty fixated on adultery." As soon as the words are out of his mouth my eyes fly to Emma and the blood rushes in my ears.

"What did you just say?" I ask.

"That Father Thomas preached the whole time—" Lee starts.

"No," I cut him off. "The last part."

"He seems pretty fixated on adultery?"

"Holy fuck," Wes says under his breath.

"What am I missing?" Lee asks.

"Adultery—" Emma says.

"A scarlet letter."

"A is for adultery," Wes says a little stunned. "We know where their lives overlapped, now I think we know what's linking them."

"Who was the woman that went out with Dennis after the last meeting?" I ask quickly hoping to God that there won't be any more victims.

"Sarah Holt," Emma says. "What would you want with that tramp?"

"Jealousy is an interesting look on you, honey. I can work with that," Lee winks.

"God you're disgusting," she says brushing his arm off of her shoulder.

"Wait, who is Sarah Holt," Wes asks.

"The brunette that was pawing all over Wes earlier," Emma answers. I look back to where the group is having dinner, but I don't see the brunette anywhere.

"Where is she?" I demand.

"Over with the rest of the group," Lee answers.

"No, she's not. Where is she?" I ask again.

"I-I-I thought I saw her go to the restroom about when you walked Anna out," Emma stutters.

I jump up and race for the bathrooms with Emma hot on my heels. That was at least thirty minutes ago, she could be long gone by now and no one would know until her body surfaces a day or two later.

Unfortunately, when I push opened the restroom door I realize we won't have to wait to recover Sarah Holt's body because she's dead on the bathroom floor with her wrists bound with rope and a large, bloody A carved into her chest.

"It looks the same," Emma whispers as she leans in to check for a pulse. "She has no pulse." But I already knew that by the vacant, faraway look in her glassy eyes.

"God damnit, not another serial killer. I really fucking hate serial killers," I say. "You stay here with her while I shut down this restaurant and get Lee and Wes started canvassing for witnesses."

"Okay," she says softly. I look back at her.

"You didn't cause this."

"I know that," she says but she won't look me in the eye, so I seriously doubt her truthfulness.

"Do you?" I ask Emma.

"Yes . . . *Mostly*."

"It's not your fault, Emma. You have a right to live your life and have human emotions like love and jealousy."

"I know," she says quietly.

"I hope you do. I'm going to go find the guys. Call it in!"

chapter 24

work, work, work

"**Y**OU WON'T BELIEVE WHAT happened!" I practically shout when I get back to the table.

"She's dead in the bathroom," Lee says looking a little devastated.

"She is," I answer Lee. "Emma is calling it in now, you two go canvas the area while I get the bar shut down for the night."

Both Wes and Lee jump out of the booth and take off at a run. Lee for the table at the front of the restaurant where all of the singles group members are sitting and Wes for the back side of the bar to see if anyone say anything that they shouldn't.

I see the manager heading towards the bar and I move as quickly as possible, so I can head him off at the pass. He's quicker than he looks and I end up chasing him down the hallway towards his office.

"Excuse me! Excuse me!" I shout.

"What?" he barks when he turns around.

"My name is Detective Claire Goodnite and I need

you to shut this building down," I demand in my take no bullshit voice.

"Excuse me but I do not think so," he growls.

"Sir, with all due respect—" I start but he cuts me off.

"No. If you had any respect at all you would respect the fact that I'm trying to run an honest business here and I don't have time for any pigs—no matter how pretty—coming in here and trying to shut me down for no reason," he huffs and I instantly don't like him.

"I wouldn't call a woman being brutally murdered by a deranged killer in your ladies room 'no reason' but who am I to judge?" I shrug. "Regardless, I don't need your permission to lock down and active crime scene."

I hear the sirens of the units Emma called coming in. I love the sound of back up. I head back down the hallway in time to hear Lee shout, "I am Captain Goodnite with the George Washington Township PD, please remain where you are and we will get to you shortly."

Several uniformed officers rush in and I have never been more excited to see them in my life. "Officers, I need you to lock this site down. Crime Scene Unit should be here shortly.

"Detective Goodnite!" Someone shouts to me. "I'm Gloria James with the George Washington Township Post, what can you tell me about this event?"

Just my luck that there would be press freaking dining here when I'm trying to handle a crime scene. But I've heard good things about Gloria so here's hoping. I've also heard Gloria—who looks to be an extremely well kept forty-five—has the hots for Lee. Worst case scenario, I'll press that for an advantage.

"Not one fucking thing, Gloria. You know the rules."

"Oh, come on! I'm locked in here and you're not going to give me anything?" She demands.

"I might give you an exclusive when this is all said and done," I warn. "Or I might not. That depends on you."

"Excellent!" she cheers. "Am I allowed to get up and make myself another martini?"

"I'm not answering that. I'm also not looking . . ."

"I got you," she laughs as she hops up and grabs a martini shaker like a pro.

I turn to walk to the door when I see the ambulance and the Crime Scene techs pull up in the body mover. I need to help them out and get them all to Emma and under her command.

"Not so fast, you fucking bitch!" I turn around just in time to dodge the fist of a very irate manager.

"I wouldn't do that if I were you," Wes growls as he grabs the manager and flips him around pinning his arms behind his back.

"And who the hell are you to get in my way?" the manager snarls.

"Her husband," Wes says point blank and I have to admit it is a tiny bit premature, but I like it. So I smile brightly at him.

"And I should care because?" the manager sneers.

"You should care because assault on a police officer and preventing them from carrying out their duties are both crimes," he informs the bar manager letting in all sink in before continuing. "And because I'm a Federal Agent."

"You've got to be fucking kidding me," the manager groans.

"I wish I were," Wes sighs before turning to a uniformed officer and saying, "I need a pair of cuffs and an escort for my dear friend here down to lock up."

"Roger that, sir," someone says.

"I have to admit that it's never a dull moment with you, Sunshine," Wes says to me with a saucy wink.

"Ha!" I laugh. "You don't know the half of it!"

"Now that this place is all sorted out, we have to go talk question Father Thomas and Father Matthew," Wes tells me.

"I know," I sigh. "I'm just having a hard time thinking that a priest could be a cold-blooded killer."

"I know that you are," he looks away, his gaze taking on a far-off quality before turning back to meet mine. "But after the weird conversation we had with Father Matthew about Father Thomas this evening and his singles group sermon on Sins of the Flesh, fornication, and all of that adultery shit we have to."

"I know it. Let's check in with Lee and Emma. Just to make sure they have everything under control and then we can head out," I tell Wes.

I take off looking for Emma and find her still in the women's restroom overseeing the loading of Sarah Holt's body on a gurney for transport. She's in her element, a force to be reckoned with, as she commands her team. I can see why Lee is so taken with her. Hell, if I were into chicks, I'd probably do her too. Emma is beautiful in a wild and windblown way as she takes command of her team ordering everyone about.

"Emma, Wes and I need to go track down a lead, do you have everything under control on this end?" I ask.

"Of course," she says as she waves me off. She doesn't even bother to look at me as she shoos me away. "I'll call you tomorrow with the autopsy results."

"Thank you!" I call out as I head back out of the bathrooms.

When I catch up to Wes he's in a hushed conversation with Lee. When I near, they both look up at me and stop all talking. That I do not care for at all.

"What's going on guys?" I ask.

"Not much, I was just telling Lee that we're about to head out to the church. He is officially in charge of wrapping up this crime scene," Wes says with a straight face and I smell bullshit. Sometimes, I'm fairly sure he uses his SERE training to evade my questions. I do not like it, I do not like it at all.

"Is that all?" I ask narrowing my eyes. I'm not sure what they're talking about, but secrets have no friends and all that.

"Of course." He smiles sweetly at me and I don't trust it for a minute.

"And these secrets have nothing to do with the current caseload?" I question.

"What secrets?" Lee asks with his own blank face.

"Don't you two use your navy ninja skills on me!" I bark. "I know what you're doing."

"We're not doing anything," Lee says innocently.

"Nothing, my ass," I grumble under my breath.

"Ready to go, Pumpkin?" Wes asks sweetly.

"Do not ever call me Pumpkin again unless you

want to get punched in yours," I snap. Wes barks out a laugh before grabbing my hand and leading me out the door before I can punch him right in his pumpkins with all thoughts of Wes and Lee and they're stupid secrets long forgotten. *For now.*

"Sure thing, Cupcake."

chapter 25

in prayer

WES KNOCKS ON THE side door, the one that leads to the living quarters for the priests just after ten o'clock. We stand on the small, dimly lit, concrete stoop for what seems like ages. In fact, we wait so long that Wes has to knock one more time.

When the door opens, Father Matthew stands there in a pair of old fashioned men's pajamas with the pants and matching button down top in a light blue with a darker blue pinstripe and piping all along the edges. The color sets off his blue eyes and shock of gray hair quite handsomely.

"Claire? Wesley? What are you doing here so late?" he questions.

"Can we come in for a second, Father?" Wes asks.

"Are you in crisis?" he asks. "Did you call off the wedding? We can pray together for guidance. Come on in."

"No nothing like that," I hedge as we make out way inside the modest apartment.

"Father Matthew, who's there?" I hear Father Thomas ask.

"Claire and Wesley," he answers as the young priest makes his way down the hallway and into the communal living area.

"Maybe we should sit down," Wes says politely.

"Yes," Father Matthews says. "Where are my manners?"

"It's fine," Wes answers.

"Can I get you all something to drink?" Father Thomas asks. "Coffee? Tea? Water?"

Since I like to make an effort not to eat or drink anything in front of anyone who might be a serial killer—especially after being poisoned by a murderer and then subdued and almost strangled by a psycho earlier this year—I decline.

"No, thank you. I'm fine," I say.

"I'm fine as well," Wes says politely.

It's times like this that I really appreciate how well trained he was by his crazy, fancy assed parents. I guess it doesn't do well to have your handsome son drinking from the finger bowl at state dinner when you're an elected official of any capacity. But whatever, he's polite when I'm tired and a little punchy and incapable of being so.

Although, it's also times like these that show me how different we can be. While Wes was being raised with a silver spoon in his mouth, Lee and I were raised to have a foam finger in one hand and a loaded hot dog in the other while screaming for the home team. Maybe his parents were right and I'm bound to embarrass them all on the campaign trail next year. Who knows?

But I still don't care. Wes and I are meant to be. If I can come to terms with it, so can his parents.

"What is this all about?" Father Matthews asks.

"Kerrigan Adams," I say softly.

"Yes," he says. "I had heard the tragic news."

"Do you know who did it?" Father Thomas asks. I narrow my eyes and tip my head to the side studying him before I voice my answer.

"Not quite yet, but we're closing in," I say confidently. He visibly swallows and looks nervous. I know it's him, in my gut I know, but I have nothing to pin it on him. "Did you know her?" I ask him.

"Of course," he says. "Kerrigan was a regular parishioner in this church. I knew her well."

"Did you now?" I ask.

"Was there anyone who paid too much attention to Kerrigan?" Wes asks the room.

"Not that I know of," answers Father Matthew. "What about you, Father Thomas?"

"Not that I know of. She was well liked all around," the other priest answers.

"She was a good girl from a good family," Father Matthews adds.

"She was," I tell him. "I've had many conversations with her parents and they're broken up about what happened."

"As I can imagine," Father Matthews says.

"And what about Dennis Boyd?" Wes asks changing the subject quickly so that we can better discover what makes the priests nervous and what does not.

"Dennis was fairly new to the church. He didn't grow up in this one like the rest of you did," Father

Thomas answers.

"He only came here after a messy divorce. Infidelity and sin make for bad bedmates in a marriage," Father Thomas says.

"Who cheated?" I ask. "Dennis or his ex?"

"I believe he did," Father Matthews answers.

"And did any of the singles group, to your knowledge, have harsh feelings towards Dennis because of his messy divorce?" Wes asks.

"No. I don't think any of them knew what had happened in his past," Father Matthew said.

"Did either of you have strong feelings about the Boyd's divorce or Dennis's infidelity?"

"Of course we have strong feelings!" Father Thomas snapped. "We're in charge of cleansing the souls of hundreds of people. We're tasked with their spiritual purity and that's nothing to be taken lightly."

"And how do you feel about Sarah Holt?" Wes asks as we both watch them closely for their reactions.

Father Matthew's eyes go wide in shock. "You can't mean?" he asks.

"Yes, Sir," Wes responds. "Sarah Holt was murdered this evening. The same way as Kerrigan Adams and Dennis Boyd."

"No," he says. "I can't believe it." Father Thomas stays quiet but pensive.

"What can you tell me about Sarah Holt?" I ask.

"She was a parishioner here and a member of our singles group," Father Matthew says.

"Had she been single long?" Wes asks.

"Yes, her last beau didn't want to get married and she hadn't found anyone in a while," Father Matthew says.

"But it wasn't for a lack of trying," Father Thomas adds not quite under his breath.

"Did you disapprove of her dating?" I ask.

"No, of course not," Father Thomas answers. "The church frowns on promiscuity."

"What Father Thomas means is that we are a bit old fashioned and like to see couples settled together for a long time, not bouncing from one mate to another. Am I right, Father Thomas," Father Matthew asks.

"Yes, Father Matthew," he responds.

"Did you know that a letter A was carved into their chests after they were murdered?" I watch Father Thomas flinch. It's subtle, almost undetected, but it was there.

"How barbaric," Father Matthew, says. "Why would someone do such a thing?"

"It is our belief that someone was branding these victims as adulterers," Wes says softly.

"And you think it was someone from this church?" Father Matthew asks incredulously.

"It's not a far reach," Wes says. "They were all members of this church, specifically the singles group."

"Do you think someone was trying to purify their spirits when they were murdered?" I press on.

"I couldn't say as I was not the one who did it," Father Thomas said.

"Where were you tonight?" I ask.

"I was here," he answers. "I spend every evening in prayer before I turn in early every night after indulging in a light supper and some evening news."

"Did you leave the church property this evening?"

Wes asks.

"No, I did not."

"How about you, Father Matthews?" Wes asks.

"I was here with Father Thomas," he answers before adding, "Also in prayer."

"Thank you," I say standing up. "We'll be in touch soon."

"Please do keep us updated," Father Matthews asks.

"We will," Wes assures him before leading me to the door.

We walk quietly through the dark parking lot with my hand held tightly in Wes's. When we climb in his car I turn to him unsure of how to express the conflicting feelings I am having.

"He's guilty," I say.

"We don't know that yet," Wes says. He's always playing Devil's Advocate and right now I'm not sure I appreciate it.

"They're not in this car, Wes. You can put away the good cop act," I say snottily.

"I'm not playing good cop," he tells me seriously. "We don't know for sure that Father Thomas is guilty. We can't go off halfcocked."

"I just . . ." I pause taking a deep breath. "I just have this feeling that something isn't right. You know?"

"I know," he tells me. "And it's important to trust your gut. I can't tell you how many times a little intuition saved mine or Lee's life in the desert. But we have to be sure before we do anything drastic."

"Yeah, I guess," I say.

"Let's go home," he says to me.

"What about my Tahoe?" I ask.

"I lifted your keys when I realized it was going to be a long night and handed them off to an agent of mine. It's probably already in the driveway." He shrugs his shoulders unrepentantly.

"That is kind of scary, Wes," I say slapping his shoulder. "I'm so impressed!"

"That's what it takes to impress you?" he asks. "Petty theft?"

"That's grand theft auto of a government vehicle, you crazy! Who does that?" I demand as he starts the car.

"You mean like when you hotwired this very government vehicle a year ago?" he asks with a raised brow.

"Uhh . . . whoops," I say cautiously. "I forgot about the time I stole the Fed-mobile."

"Yeah, whoops," he says sarcastically as he drives through town.

"In my defense, I had a good excuse," I defend my actions.

"What excuse?" he practically shouts in the dark car.

"You were about to get Lee to fire me!" I shout right back.

"So, committing a fairly serious crime was how you combated almost getting fired?" he laughs. "I'm not sure I am ever going to understand your logic and reasoning no matter how long we'll be married," Wes says as he pulls into the driveway next to my department SUV.

"That's wild," I say getting out of the car.

"Keys should be in the mailbox," he says. I walk out to the curb and open the mailbox and sure enough, there they are.

"Well, I'll be damned," I muse.

"Come on," he says. "It's been a long day and an even longer night. I think a hot shower and then as much sleep as we can pack into an hour or two is in store."

"It's barely midnight and we don't have to be up until six," I remind him. "How did you get only an hour or two of sleep?"

"Easy," he smiles that slow lazy grin that has always turned my belly to mush and usually means exciting things. "I'm going to walk you upstairs to our bedroom and strip you down, that might take ten minutes, then I'm going to fuck you in the shower, that might take an hour. After that we'll actually need to shower so that's another thirty minutes. And then I'm going to take you to bed and make love to you until we both forget how awful life can be. Then we'll sleep. You good with that?"

"I'm good with that," I answer on a nod which makes his gorgeous smile flash that much wider.

"Fantastic," he says before touching his mouth to mine in a hard, quick kiss. That's actually one of my favorite of his kisses, the quick lip touch that means so much more and usually proceeds fantastic things.

Wes takes me by the hand and leads me up the walk to the front door. Without dropping his grip on my hand, he shuffles his keys in his free hand and gracefully unlocks the door, pushing it open for me to walk inside. After he passes through the entryway behind me, he shuts and locks the door before leading me up the stairs.

When we hit our room at the end of the hall, we each slide our sidearms out of our holsters—his hidden, mine not—and lock them up for the night before as previously promised, Wes pulls my t-shirt over my head.

He takes my hand again and walks us into the bathroom where he reaches in the shower and turns the water on to warm up. His coat is long gone but he pulls the knot in his tie loose before letting it slip through his fingers. He takes my hand in his and gently wraps the blue striped silk around my wrist, not tying it tight, but letting it slip free.

"One day I'm going to bind you with my ties—naked to the bed," he tells me in his whiskey smooth voice. "And then I'll eat you until you beg me to stop and then I'll fuck you until we both can't take it anymore. What do you have to say about that?"

"Okay," I whisper. His smirk is ridiculous as he unbuttons his crisp white shirt. I often wonder of it's in a handbook somewhere that the Fed suit can only be equipped with a white button-down shirt because they all wear the same one. Only Wes makes it look oh so good.

"I thought you'd be onboard," he says as he pops the button on my jeans. The zipper rasps loudly in contrast to the running water through the otherwise quiet room.

Wes does not push my jeans and panties down but instead slides his palm flat inside my panties and down my mound. He runs the tip of his index finger through my slit and I practically come out of my skin.

"You're always so fucking wet for me," he growls circling my clit with his finger.

"Yes," I say as he slides two fingers deep inside me and pumps them in and out until I'm arching against him and clawing at his shoulders.

Only then does he slide his hand free to the sound of my whimpers and pushes my jeans and panties to the floor. Wes unsnaps my bra and tosses it to the ground leaving me there to stand totally naked as I watch him pull the belt free from his slacks and drop it to the ground before lowering his zipper and letting the dark material fall to the floor unceremoniously. His amber eyes never leave mine as he hooks his fingertips into the waistband of his dark gray boxer briefs and shoves them to the ground letting his heavy cock spring free.

"Come here, baby," he says with his voice gruff and I do not hesitate to jump in his arms in time for him to lower his mouth to mine. I open underneath his and he licks in.

He does not move his mouth from mine as he backs into the shower dragging me along with him in the very best of ways. I gasp when the warm water hits my skin and Wes glides his rough hands up and down my sides, warming me up from the inside out.

Slowly, Wes turns me around to face away from him. I tip my head back and enjoy the way the warm water sprays on my skin and loosens my muscles. I hear the cap on the body wash bottle pop open as he squirts some in his hands and then I feel his heavy palms land gently on top of my shoulders as he works the lather into my skin in small, slow circles.

Inch by inch, Wes moves his hands across my shoulders and down my arms working every kink in my body out. And then he presses the length of his hard body against my back. He works his hands slowly up the sides of my waist needing and massaging as he goes until he reaches my full breasts. Wes cups one in each hand, circling my nipples with his thumbs and I arch my back pushing further into his hands when he pinches them hard in between his thumbs and index fingers.

Wes wraps one arm around my belly pulling me tight against him while he slides his other palm down, down, down until he circles my clit with his index finger. I try to wiggle against him for more friction, more anything, but he's holding me so tight that I can't move. I can only take what Wes will give me and he's giving me everything.

I look down and watch as Wes pushes his hand down even further and slides two fingers deep inside me, his thumb taking over on my clit. My body is on fire and I'm burning up from the inside out. I desperately try to grind against his hand as he pumps his fingers in and out.

"Wes—" I cry out.

"That's it, baby. It's mine and I want it. All you have to do is give it to me," he rumbles in my ear as he uses his hand to push me over the edge.

Wes loosens his hold on me so that I can catch my breath and I turn around to face him. He looks into my eyes, watching me watch him as he slowly raises his fingers to his mouth and sucks them in deep. When he slips them from his lips he tangles his fingers in my hair at the back of my head and crushes his mouth to mine. I open up underneath him and he plunges his tongue inside. The taste of the heady combination of him and me and my body heats again.

Wes presses me back into the shower wall and the stone tiles are cool on my skin. He wraps his hand firmly down my thigh and lifts it to press high on his hip. My muscles burn as they stretch and the movement opens me up to feel his hard length rub against my most intimate places.

He slides his other hand out of my hair and down my side to my other thigh lifting me up high on the wall. I let out an undignified squeak until the noise is abruptly cut short by the feeling of the tip of his cock at my entrance.

And then he makes good on his earlier promise to fuck me in the shower as he thrusts deep inside me. I gasp at the fast intrusion. Wes doesn't give me time to adjust before he's moving hard and fast in and out of my body.

This is one of my favorite things about being with Wes—like this—together. That he can be sweet and tender or dirty and a little wild, either way there is a connection that is made between us in the moment and I revel in the feeling of the slip and slide of his cock inside me.

Wes plunges in and out of my body harder and harder as he takes my mouth and the feeling is overwhelming. I have to break my mouth away from his to try and catch my breath, crying out. I feel my body clench around him as his movements become more frantic. We're both riding the knife's edge right now, so close to falling over and we both know it.

"Claire—" he groans as he moves within me, over me.

"Yes," I call out as he pushes me over the edge right along with him.

After a moment, Wes pulls out and then lowers my shaky legs to the shower floor. Otherwise we stay wrapped up completely in each other. My heart is still pounding when he pushes my wet hair out of my face so gently, tenderly even, with his rough hands.

Wes lowers his mouth to mine again, but this time it's sweet, tender, and short. When he leans back he pulls the hair tie holding my long hair up in a messy bun out, letting it fall around my shoulders like a wet mop. I must have made a face when it fell because Wes laughs.

"This is one of the things I love about you," he says so softly that I almost don't hear it.

"That I look like a drowned rat in the shower?"

"That this has never changed in some ways. You've always had this massive amount of long, black hair. Paired with those eyes, and baby you take my breath away." My heart fills. I know that he loves me, but Wes isn't a man of many words. For him to speak like this I know that he not only means it, but that it's important for him that I know how he feels.

"Wes—" I say, my emotions clogging my throat.

"And that ass doesn't hurt either," he says, and I laugh. Message received. Wes thinks I'm special, but we don't need to wax poetic about it for all time. That's just not his style.

Wes reaches for the shampoo bottle and pours some

into his palm. He works a lather between his hands before working the soap into my hair. His strong fingers massage my scalp and I can't help but let out a little growl making him chuckle. Wes tips my head back into the water to rinse the suds free before washing his own hair. When he ducks his head into the running water, Wes pops out and shakes his head like a dog making me scream.

"Wes!"

"What, baby," he laughs.

"Nothing, you mutt," I laugh too. "I just love you."

"I love you too, Claire," he pauses soaping up his body to say before shutting of the water.

Wes trails a towel over every inch of my body, even squeezing the water out of my hair before quickly drying himself off. He neatly hangs the towel back on the rack before scooping me up in his arms like a bride and carrying me to our bed.

Where he drops me like a rock.

"Wes!" I shout but he covers me with his hard body and then smiling, he covers my mouth with his.

He kisses his way down my body stopping to nip and then suck on the side of my neck before soothing the hurt with soft open-mouthed kisses. He trails his lips, slightly parted down my throat and over my chest and down to my breast. He licks my nipple and I arch into him as he sucks it in deep into his mouth. He circles my other nipple with the tip of his index finger, his nail scraping lightly. And then he lets my nipple got with a pop.

He slides back up my body and kisses me hungrily before I press on his shoulders to have him sit down in the middle of the bed. I climb on his lap, straddling him. I like being this way with Wes, face to face, nose to nose, because I can see everything he's feeling, every emotion as it flashes across his face.

I rise up on my knees before sliding down his cock. I slip my legs out from underneath me and wrap them around Wes's waist. He pulls his knees up to better balance and we sit like that wrapped around each other touching and kissing. Here, like this, there is no rough fucking but gently rocking together. His cock deep inside me as his body rubs against my clit.

Here Wes fulfills his last promise to me, to make love to me until we both forget that anything exists outside of him and me.

When at last we come together like a wave gently cresting over my skin, Wes rolls us to lie down in our bed. He pulls the blankets over us and just as gently he whispers, "I love you," before we drift off to sleep.

Run!

I'm running as fast as my little feet will take me through the woods behind my parents' house. I have to get away from the bad man. If he catches me now, I'll never get away. I have to be free.

Run! I have to run faster.

I see the blue gray light as it spills through the trees. Mommy always told me this was her favorite part of the day—looking at the sun as it comes up in the morning. I ran away late in the night when the bad man was sleeping. It was my only chance. After he broke the lock on the closet door I knew that I had a chance to get out.

Free.

I'm free. That's the words in my head as the trees break and I see Wes standing at the edge of the back-yard. I'm free. I'm finally free. Wes looks up and he sees me.

"I've got her!" he shouts to someone.

My heart is beating so hard in my chest and it hurts to breathe. I'm so tired but I have to keep running. I see Wes, his face, I know that he'll protect me. Wes always protects me. He will keep me safe. He will keep me free.

I push my feet just a little harder, I run just a little faster. I'm almost there. I'm almost free when I get to the clearing where I saw Wes standing just up ahead, only he's not there anymore. Or he is. Wes isn't standing, he's lying on the ground covered with blood.

There is blood all around the ground and the trees drip with the sticky stuff. I have never seen so much blood and I want to be sick. But when I look to Wes for help, his eyes are open on his beautiful face but he doesn't see anything because my beautiful Wes is dead and it's all my fault.

"No!" I scream.

And I know that I'll never be free. Not ever again.

No! Not Wes. Not now. I scam. The tears burn hot down my cheeks and my heart is breaking, no, it's not broken, it's shattered into a million pieces that will never be put back together again.

"Shh," someone whispers. "You're alright, honey."

"Wes?" I ask but that's not quite right, he's dead. I saw him die.

"It was a dream, baby," he explains, and I force open my eyes.

"You're here?" I ask, and I hate that my voice sounds so small.

"Yeah, honey. It was just a dream," he tells me. "Do you want to talk about it?"

I stop and think about it, I have never told Wes about any of my dreams before, only Anna. I do not ever tell anyone else about them. I can tell he's holding his breath too—probably thinking he's about to be turned down. Again. But I'm not, this time is different because it feels so different to me.

"Yeah," I say softly. "I do."

"I dream this same dream all the time," I explain. "It's back when I'm running away. I'm running through the woods and I have to go faster and faster because I don't want the bad man to catch me. I can't go back to the closet—"

"Wait," he says. "You're remembering?"

"Anna thinks it might be memories, but they come differently every time, so I don't know."

"What do you mean?" he asks. "Explain please."

"Well, like this one—" I start.

"Wait, are there more than one?" he asks me.

"Yes, I dream about being taken, a closet, I'm assuming I was kept in one, running away, and when you rescued me," I finish softly.

"Anything else?"

"I dream about the . . . *abuse*."

Wes is quiet for a long moment and I wonder if he doesn't really want to know which I'm not afraid to admit kind of stings. He has been badgering me for months to tell him what my nightmares are about and now that he has a tiny glimpse at my hell, he doesn't want to know. That makes me feel small and unimportant and I don't like it at all. I brush those feelings off and stuff them away for a really bad day.

"You said they change?" he asks. "How so?"

"Like I was saying, this one is the one where I'm running away and you save me. I see you through the trees just up ahead and I hear you call out to Lee that you've got me."

"Yeah," he says. "That really happened."

"Usually I dream that you grab me and I pass out, that's when I wake up," I explain.

"That's what really happened, honey," he says softly. "I really think you're remembering. You're working through something and it's just out of reach."

"Yes!" I shout. I'm getting excited that Wes seems to understand. "It's like the answers are just under the icy top of a frozen lake. I know that they're there but I still can't get to them."

"What else do you dream about that day?" he asks me.

"Sometimes, I dream that the bad man catches up to me and I never make it back to you," I whisper into the dark.

"I'm so sorry," he says. "But you should know that there is nothing I wouldn't do to find you, to get you back. There is no distance too far. I love you too much. I will always find you, honey."

"This time, I dreamed that when I got to you, you were dead and lying in a pool of blood," I say as fast as I possibly can. I hate the taste of the words in my mouth.

"I'm right here, Claire," he says as he takes my hand and places my palm to lay flat on his chest. "I'm alive and right here and I'm not going anywhere," he says resolutely.

"I know that," I explain. "And I really do, but I can't help but feel like something is wrong."

"What do you mean?"

"Maybe it's a bad omen or something, but I can't help but feel like something really bad is about to happen," I explain.

"You can't think like that," he tells me. "This case is really bad. It's ugly and it's messy, but you can't go through life waiting for the other shoe to drop."

"I know that." And I do, I really do, but still. I can't help how I feel.

"Do you?" Wes questions.

"Yes," I tell him. "But you need to listen to me, Wes. Something is really wrong here. I can feel it in my bones."

"I think it's been a really long week and you're overworked and tired. I think you're really worried about your friends and your bonehead brother is being an idiot so you have a lot on your plate. Let's just go back to sleep and when we wake up in the morning, everything will seem better."

"Okay," I say quietly like the kid who just got a dressing down from the principal, but I can't help but feel like agreeing with Wes is making a huge fucking mistake. It's too bad that later would prove how wrong we really were. Only then it would be too late.

chapter 26

BEEP . . . BEEP . . . BEEP . . .
Wes's alarm sounds on his nightstand and this morning I can't help but feel like everything is about to change. He reaches over and shuts the alarm off before turning to me.

"You okay, baby?" he asks me.

"I don't think so," I say hesitantly. More than anything, I don't want to go back to the days where Lee and Wes think I'm incapable of handling my duties. And even more than that I don't want him to know that I am visited by nightmares almost every night now. That I tossed and turned all night after I told him about my dreams that seem to be turning into memories.

"Everything is fine," he says. "Nothing is going to go wrong today."

"You can't say that!" I shout jumping up from the bed.

"Claire, be rational," he says firmly.

"Excuse me?" I ask. Wes couldn't possibly be insinuating that I am acting crazy.

"Claire—" he starts.

"I'm not crazy!" I shout sounding even to myself like anything but sane or rational.

"I never said that you were," he snaps.

"You didn't seem to be implying that I'm not either," I tell him as I fold my arms across my chest.

"I'm sorry," he says. "I just don't want you upset." I sigh. That makes sense. I'm not sleeping well and that coupled with the stress of this case is making me a little frazzled.

"I'm sorry too," I say softly.

"Come here, baby," he says, and I walk over to him letting him pull me into his arms. "Everything is going to be okay." I just nod, but as we get ready for work I can't help but feel like there is a dark cloud hanging overhead. I still feel like something is really, really wrong.

I drive to work thinking dark thoughts so it's incredibly fitting that it rains.

This morning, Wes and I did not touch or fool around as we got dressed. The intimacy between us was lost, not for forever, but for the moment. He thinks I'm worried about nothing, but I can't help but think I have everything to worry about.

I showered by myself, waiting until after he was done with his own shower to step in and then dressed silently by myself. I have no doubt that he waited for me to join him in the shower like we do every morning because he took the world's longest shower for a man. But I just couldn't even though my heart ached to join him, to have him hold me in his arms. I know it makes me sound weak, but I needed him to hear me, to hear my worries and my fears, and to help me through them, not just brush them aside. Shit, I've been friends with Anna for so long that now I need to be a sharer. I can't wait to tell her, I bet she's going to love the shit out of that.

I can't top the sinking feeling in my stomach that something is very wrong. That I'm missing something. I have to stop Father Thomas before he hurts anymore people, but how?

As I pull into the parking lot the ringing of my phone breaks me out of my head.

"Goodnite," I answer as I pull into my spot in the back.

"Hey," Anna says when I answer. "It's me."

"Hey, yourself." I smile glad to hear my friend's voice this morning.

"I . . . I just wanted to call and check in," she says softly.

"Is everything okay?" I ask.

"Yeah," she sighs. "I'm just feeling a little silly after I freaked out and bailed last night," she explains. I can hear in her voice that she is uneasy with the situation, maybe even unsure and that is the exact opposite of how I would usually describe Anna. That simple fact makes me mad at my dipshit brother all over again.

"Well, you missed all the fun," I tell her.

"Oh yea?" she asks. "How so?"

"Well, Sarah Holt was murdered by the killer. Probably right after you left."

"You're kidding?" she asks shedding her weird feelings from the previous night and in an instant assuming her professional role.

"I wish I were. Same MO as Dennis Boyd and Kerrigan Adams."

"That's awful," she says, and I can hear her shudder. I do too because it *is* awful.

"We had to shut down the bar. The manager was a real asshole and tried to take a swing at me."

"How did that make you feel?" she asks me, falling into shrink mode and I realize that I have missed our chats. As I've been letting Wes in more it doesn't mean I can't talk to Anna too. I can have them both.

"It pissed me off, but Wes grabbed him before he could and arrested him. It was awesome!" I cheer, and she laughs.

"That is awesome," she laughs. "Go Wes!"

"Then Wes and I went to the church to talk to Father Thomas. I know it's him I just can't get anything that will stick," I can hear the frustration in my own voice. After a slight pause, Anna speaks.

"What makes you so sure that it's Father Thomas?" she asks me.

"Well, everyone said he preached about sins of the flesh and all that. Plus, he talked about Dennis Boyd's divorce and all that," I explain. "I just do, damn it."

"But I'm not sure that makes him guilty," Anna says softly.

I sigh. "Fuck. I know it. I'm losing sight of what's

important, but I can't help but feel like something bad is about to happen."

"I'm sure it'll be fine," she says.

"Yeah," I say. "You're right. Wes said the same thing this morning." And isn't that really the crux of the problem? Everyone keeps saying everything will be fine and no one is listening to me say I have a very bad feeling.

"I'll call and check in later, maybe we'll go to dinner. Just us?" she asks me.

"Sure, I'd like that," I tell her before she hangs up and I sigh again. There seems to be a lot of sigh worthy moments this morning. Maybe Wes is right, it's not a bad omen, but a culmination of a shit case, a wedding to plan, and my brother tearing apart our social group with his wayward dick.

But even as I think it, I know that's not it.

"We have a winner!" Emma shouts when the metal elevator doors ding open and I can't help but laugh. "Come on down!"

"You're ridiculous," I tell her.

"You already know this," she says.

"So, you called me down here because…?" I ask.

I was sitting at my desk with my umpteenth cup of coffee of the morning and an ulcer that is most definitely

developing in my gut looking over all of my case notes and trying to find anything I can on Father Thomas when the phone on my desk rang.

"Goodnite," I answered.

"The results are in," Emma barks into the phone. "Get your ass down here." And then she hangs up.

I sighed in frustration for the millionth time this morning when the dots wouldn't connect. I can't help but feel like a Sword of Damocles is hanging over my head. Like a clock is ticking down the seconds and I'm running out of time. So, I push back from my rickety desk and head for the elevator to be greeted by Emma who is obviously feeling the strain as well. She's not a big fan of serial killers either.

"What do you got?" I ask her.

"Autopsy results," she says taking on a more serious demeanor.

"Anything unusual?" I ask her.

She sighs. "I really wish there were. Should I just run the highlights for you and email you the report?"

"Yeah," I say. I hate this shit.

"Alright, highlight reel: Sarah Holt was struck on the side of the head but that is not what killed her. More than likely it subdued them so that the killer could bind them with the jute. Fibers were found in the wounds on her wrists confirm it is jute."

"I don't understand why Father Thomas is beating the victims over the head to subdue them," I muse aloud. "He seems young and pretty fit."

"He does," Emma adds. "But what if it's not him?

What if it's one of the members of the singles group? That probably fits the profile better anyways although you'd have to check with Anna for that."

"True."

"So back to the highlights?" she asks me.

"Yeah, sorry," I murmur.

"Sarah Holt was stabbed through the heart and then repeatedly several times before the letter A was carved into her chest. She was still warm but dead when we got to her so that was shortly before we found her, I'd say ten minutes or so."

"Thanks, Emma," I tell her before heading back upstairs to my desk.

I call the bar and ask for their security camera footage. Emma is right, Sarah Holt had to have been murdered just before we found her, so the killer would be on those tapes.

"*Cicada Bar and Grill,*" someone answers.

"Yes, I'm Detective Goodnite with the George Washington Township PD," I say. "I'd like to speak to the owner."

"*This is the owner and we don't talk to cops here,*" he says in a gruff voice.

Unfortunately, it seems, that the bar owner shares the same sentiments about law enforcement that the manager does.

"There was a murder at your restaurant last night, I need to see the security camera footage," I tell him.

"*Well, then you can bring me a God damned Search Warrant or you ain't getting shit, lady,*" he barks into the phone. "*And let me tell you, you and your Fed aren't welcomed here either.*" And then he hangs up.

"God damnit!" I shout as I slam down the receiver. Doesn't anyone care that there is a serial killer on the loose. You would think more people would be willing to do something as trivial as hand over some stupid security tapes to help out.

My phone rings again. I sigh and answer it, "Good-nite."

And then everything goes to shit just like I knew it would.

chapter 27

sanctuary

"**I** KNOW IT'S YOU!" she says as she chases me through the sanctuary.

I just smile at her.

"You have everyone looking at Father but it's you." I shake my head and smile indulgently at the petite brunette like she's a small child. "You killed Kerrigan and you killed Dennis and you killed Sarah."

"Is that so?" I ask as I inch closer to her.

"Yes, it is and I can prove it!"

"And how is that?" I ask.

"I'm a psychologist for the police department, I put together profiles," she says triumphantly. "And I checked around, I can prove that your alibis are nothing but lies."

"Like what?" I ask as I edge closer to her still. She doesn't seem to realize how near to each other we are, and I revel in the hunt.

"You were at the bistro the other night. I saw you on my way out and I didn't realize it at the time because *you were dressed in street clothes, but it was you. I realize that now . . . What are you doing? She asks but it's too late. I swing my arm out clipping her across the face with an ornate gold cross.*

The woman falls in a heap and I love the poetic justice of this sacrifice being made at the Lord's altar. I pull her body up to the steps at the front and pull the piece of jute out of my pocket. I carry it with me everywhere. It's the very same one that I used to bind everyone's wrists together so that I could do the work that I set out to do.

"'The woman was dressed in purple and scarlet, and was glittering with gold, precious stones and pearls. She held a golden cup in her hand, filled with abominable things and the filth of her adulteries.' You could have been many things but instead you chose to be a whore just like them," I whisper into her ear the words of Revelations as she begins to wake.

I hear a noise near the doors and I know that this will have to be quick. I won't be able to savor this sacrifice like I did the others. This will be my last act in the service of our Lord and I take my blade in both hands one last time raising it up over my head

"Police!" Claire. "Don't move!

But I do move without hesitation. The knife arcs through the air and plunges into Anna's heart. I watch her face as every emotion flits across her face. I hope she's happy now. She looks of panic, of desperation, and then as it changed into resignation. She knows now that she is dying. My work is finished. My mission has been fulfilled.

And then I hear the gunshots blast through the sanctuary . . .

chapter 28

man to man

Wes

A BAD OMEN. That's what the superstitious guys on the old teams would call what Claire described this morning.

When she woke up in my arms this morning screaming at the top of her lungs still gripped in the clutches of one of those fucking awful nightmares, she said something felt off, *wrong even*. I didn't tell her at the time, but I felt it too. Something is wrong, I just don't know what.

I'm standing at the window in my office trying to wrap my mind around the demons that chase my girl at night, the ones I can't see. I would give anything, *do anything*, to spare her from those nightmares which are coming more and more often.

There's a knock on my office door.

"Come in," I bark out and in walks Lee. He looks like shit, but then I guess if I were in his shoes, I probably would too.

"Well if it isn't Deputy Dipshit," I greet him in a man hug and slap him on the back. "What's up, brother? You look like hammered horse shit," I laugh.

"Thanks." He rolls his eyes. "I really appreciate your undying loyalty."

"Anytime," I respond. "So, what brings you to my neck of the woods?"

"I need advice," he says and by the look on his face, he would rather eat a bag of nails and be anywhere else in the world than here having this conversation with me.

And again, I can't blame him.

"What's going on?" I ask.

"I'm in love with her," he says. "I'm in love with Emma and she hates me."

"It definitely seems like that's the case," I tell him.

"Thanks for sugar coating that for me, man. It really helps." he snarks before asking, "What do I do?"

"I wish I knew, Lee. I really do. But I kind of agree with your sister, I'm not sure you can overcome this love triangle situation. It might be best to just walk away," I tell Lee honestly. I know it's not what he wants to hear but maybe it's what he needs to hear. Things are in pretty sore shape right now and we have a murderer to catch.

"No!" he shouts. "That's out of the question."

"Then you have to make things right with Anna before you continue to pursue things with Emma. But I would be upfront with her and tell her that you're trying to right those wrongs and be a better man," I tell him. At least that's what I would do if I were in his shoes.

"That's a good plan," he says. "Did my sister make you this touchy feely?" he asks me.

"Hell no!" I laugh. "Claire would hand me my balls in a paper cup first."

"She's a tough cookie but underneath it all she's just a big softy," he tells me.

"I know." I smile at my best friend. "She's the best thing that ever happened to me."

"Don't worry," he says. "She knows." I throw my head back and laugh.

"So, you think talking it out will work?" he asks me looking—for the first time in any that I can remember—worried. Not even when we were dodging enemy fire or hunting down the baddest of the bad in some far off, war torn nation, did I ever see Lee look worried. In fact, he was eerily calm before, during, and after those missions.

"I don't know," I tell him honestly. "But with women, the one you love in particular, full transparency is usually best."

"So you tell Claire everything?" he asks.

"Everything that matters," I tell him seriously when my phone rings. "Yeah?" I say when I pick up the phone. "*Anna's at the church. She says she knows who the killer is,*" Claire's panicked voice comes through the line. Jesus this doesn't sound good.

"Lee's here. We're on our way." I end the call abruptly and jump up from my seat.

"What's up?" Lee asks instantly alert.

"Claire just called," I tell him as I grab my keys. "Anna's at the church she says she knows who the killer is. We gotta roll." I'm running out the door but he's right behind me. Just like old times.

We jump in my car and I'm peeling out of the parking lot. We're probably the closest to the church from everyone else. Here's hoping we can stop Anna from doing something stupid. At least that's what I'm praying for anyways.

"This is all my fault," Lee says from my passenger seat.

"Brother. Now is not the time to freak out," I warn.

"You're right. She's smart. She'll be smart," he chants but I can't help but feel like Claire's nightmare was right, in that everything is about to go to straight to shit. I had a sixth sense overseas when an op was about to go tits up, we all did really. It was the only way to stay alive and it hasn't left me since. I feel the same tingling along the back of my neck when a case is not what it seems, and I have to fight against scratching at the back of my neck now.

I cannot believe that Anna would try and solve this herself. This killer is dangerous. But she was so sure she could show Lee that she is his equal, that she's good enough for him. The truth is she was always better than him. I love Lee like a brother but he's been a real ass where these two women are concerned.

Unfortunately, she couldn't see that somewhere along the way, while she was falling in love with Lee, he was falling for Emma. What a cluster fuck. I pull into the parking lot of the church on two wheels and throw it in park before Lee and I are out and running. Hell, Lee bailed out and was running before the car had stopped. That's how urgent the situation is, or SNAFU, Situation Now All Fucked Up, as we would say. I see

Claire heading for the church from the other end of the parking lot. We are running full out, but nothing would prepare us for what we would encounter when we entered the sanctuary.

And then Claire screams . . .

chapter 29

Anna

I'M RUNNING.

"Goodnite," I answer. "*I'm at the church. I know who it is come quick*," Anna whispers into the phone when I answer the phone just before the click sounds telling me that she ended the call abruptly. I pick up my phone and dial Wes, "*Yeah*," he says when he picks up. "Anna's at the church. She says she knows who the killer is."

"*Lee's here. We're on our way.*" And then he ends the connection. I pick up my phone one more time and dial Emma. "Anna's at the church. She says she knows who it is. I'm on my way there now," I say when she picks up the phone. "*Fuck!*" she bites out. "*I'm on my way.*" I'm running to my SUV by the time I hang up with Emma I'm climbing in and turning the key. I am probably the farthest away from the church. Praying I get there in time and so fucking angry that Anna would try and solve this herself. This killer is dangerous. But she was so sure she could show my dumb fucking brother that she's a contemporary.

She couldn't see that somewhere along the way, while she was falling in love with Lee, he was falling for Emma. Or she didn't *want* to see it. This is just a big fucking mess. I pull into the parking lot of the church and barely have the Tahoe in park before I'm running for the church doors with the car door hanging open. Lee and Wes are heading for the church from the other end of the lot. Somehow, I made it here before them but then again, I did break land speed records to do it. We all are in hot pursuit, but nothing would prepare us for what we would encounter when we entered the sanctuary.

I'm running as fast as I can, pushing my body as hard as I can. From the minute I hung up the phone from talking to Anna, I knew that she was going to do something stupid. How could she? The answer is simple, she wants to belong that badly, to be worthy of someone like Lee whether he was in love with her or not.

"You take the front, I'll go around back," Emma says. She has her gun pulled as well. We are a small township but even the Medical Examiner is trained to handle an intense situation.

"Got it," I say. "Wes and Lee should be here any minute, they were right behind us."

As I run up the steps, I pull my sidearm from its holster and steady my arms. I breathe in three times and out one to center my focus. It's some SEAL trick Lee taught me ages ago and it helps. I push open the big double door and enter the sanctuary. I draw my sidearm when I hear Anna's scream.

Nothing could prepare me for what I was about to see.

"What have you done?" I hear Father Thomas scream from the side but I can't look at him now.

"Police!" I shout. "Don't move!

But Father Matthew does with a maniacal look on his face. The knife arcs through the air and plunges into Anna's heart. Until the day I die, I will never forget the look of panic, of desperation on her face as it changed into resignation. She knows. And then I pull the trigger over and over again. I empty my magazine into Father Matthew's body until he falls limp to the side. I never would have guessed that the calm and quiet priest who told Wes and I we were a lost cause, who practically pointed every finger at Father Thomas, had killed four people in the name of God.

Pain.

What a stupid little word to describe what I am feeling right now—just four fucking letters—such a mundane word to explain the white-hot lightning rips through my torso in the vicinity of where my heart used to be. It sears so acutely that my breath catches in my throat.

"No!" someone screams. I think it was me. It might have been me, but I don't know.

Hands grab me from behind to stop me from closing the gap between me and the bloody body on the altar steps of my family church. These slabs of muscle, bone, joint, and tendons restrain me, they hold me back from the jarring loss. But the cold truth of what has come to pass is front and center for all to see. They pull the now empty, wasted piece of steel and lead from my hands and toss it behind them.

Lee pushes Father Mathew's body away to the side. Emma rushes in from the back and drops to her knees by Anna's side and unties her hands. Emma is leaning over a prone Anna on the steps to the altar.

Blood covers them both. "Anna! God damnit stay with me," Emma shrieks as she tries to stop the blood flowing so freely from slices and holes places all over her petite body. I drop to my knees beside her. "What can I do? Tell me what to do!""Just stop the bleeding."*Anguish.*

This is anguish. This severe pain. A wound licked raw that I know will never heal. This is a wound that will only fester and turn putrid.

Before I had looked at victims and thought why can't I save them? Or it should have been me. But looking at the shell of what had been as it's splayed on the plush carpet of the altar steps I know without a doubt that I would trade places in a heartbeat. If only it was my blood that was spilled and not hers.

"Emma," Anna rasps. There's a rattling behind her voice and everyone in this room know what that means. *A death rattle.*"Save your energy, babe," Emma tells her sweetly."I see it now," she says. "It was wrong of me to want him. He was always yours."

"No," Emma denies as the tears stream down her beautiful face. "Don't say that."

"Love him for me." My breath seizes in my lungs and my own tears burn behind my eyes.

"No. You do it because I won't!" Emma sobs.

"He loves you," Anna rattles.

"I don't care," Emma lies.

"He's going to . . . to need someone to . . . to love him." I can see that it's taking all of her energy to get her last wishes out.

"No, Anna," Emma pleads. "Anything but that."

"Just . . . love him." And then her eyes dip closed never to open again as the last of her breath rattles out of her body. "Anna!" Emma cries. I'm stunned. I'm in shock. And I don't know what to do. "Emma, honey," Liam says as he reaches for her. "No!" she screams as she pulls away. "Don't touch me!""Emma," I call out unsure of what to do. "No, Lee. This is all your fault." Liam looks as if he has been struck. "Emma, you can't mean that," he pleads.

"She wanted so badly to belong to you, to fit into your world and that pushed her straight to this moment," Emma says with an eerie coldness in her voice.

"Emma," Lee calls out again. "Do me a favor, Lee and just stay the fuck away from me." And then she storms outside.

Wes grabs me from behind again and pulls me away from my friend. The only person I would turn to when the road turned dark. How many nights did she talk me through a terror I couldn't see myself through alone? Too many to count.

"Let me go!" I wail. My voice is harsh and raw. The words are ripped from my chest leaving a raw wound in its wake.

"No," someone says. I don't know who. I don't care either, but I think it may be Wes. I can't stop staring at the broken remains of someone I had loved above all else. Someone who managed to do the unthinkable, to break down my walls and invade my heart.

Grief.

If this is what grief feels like I don't want it. I want to go back to this morning when my life was normal. I had had the world at my feet, and my family was whole. I feel raw . . . *exposed* . . . I'm a wound that's been flayed open down to the bone. But it cannot be stitched or cauterized.

Maybe this is shock. I don't know. All I do know is that the world is a darker place tonight. This is not a loss that I or anyone else will get over. Not now, not ever.

Everything has changed.

epilogue

end of watch

COLD.

I walk into the Civic Center feeling cold and empty. I flash my badge to the officer guarding the door, but everyone here knows who I am and why I'm here. The seats are all empty but one. Lee sits in the corner in neither the front nor the back. Not wanting to bother him in his grief or willing to talk to anyone, I sit in the back.

Anna's flag draped coffin sits at the front on a wooden stand with a uniformed officer standing guard on either side. While Anna may have felt like she didn't belong to us, that she was never a part of the department since she acted only as a contractor, but in the end the department was there for her, insisting on full burial honors, which for someone without a badge is almost unheard of.

Lee needed no persuading having agreed whole-heartedly. His guilt at casting her aside is riding him hard.

I don't even know why I am here, I guess I just needed to be near her one last time to get my head on straight before her funeral in the morning. At home I was restless. I couldn't sleep. I didn't even know how to try.

The last week has been a nightmare of a media circus. Not to mention coming to terms with the fact that the priest who baptized Lee and I turned out to be a psychopath on a murderous rage. I was right when I said Father Thomas didn't have to subdue his victims to tie them up. I was also wrong because he wasn't the killer. To which I owed him a huge apology that he accepted graciously. He really is a nice guy.

It turns out after we spoke on the phone, Anna realized that she recognized Father Matthew in plain clothes walking into the Cicada Street Bar and Grill as she was leaving. Instead of telling Wes, Lee, or myself, she decided to prove once and for all that she was part of the team. But having no training, she didn't know that rule number fucking one is never go in unarmed and without backup.

Anna made a fatal mistake that day and for it we're all suffering the consequences. Lee and Emma in particular. After being unable to stay away from Lee despite her friendship with Anna, Emma is now torn up with grief and blames Lee for everything. To my knowledge, she has not spoken to him since the day Anna died. Lee, who is so in love with Emma that he pushed and pushed her regardless of Anna's feelings is now back to square one. Where before he had Emma in secret in his bed, now he has absolutely nothing and according Wes, is unraveling at an alarming pace.

As for me, I don't know where to start. I can't make heads or tails of my feelings. I have cried more in the last week than I have in years. The worst part is, the nightmares aren't a maybe anymore but happen like clockwork every night, sometimes several a night. I can't help but think that without being able to talk them through with Anna I won't be able to overcome them. Three years ago, a visit with a department shrink was the last thing I needed or wanted. Yet somehow, she had become one of the most important people in my life and now there is an empty spot in my heart that can never be filled or repaired.

I don't know how long I have sat here when Wes slides into the seat next to mine. I turn into his arms and smell the spicy scent that is inherently Wes. I bury my face in his t-shirt and just breathe it in finding comfort in him.

"I thought I would find you here," he says to me. Wes looks adorably rumpled in a pair of gray sweatpants that say *NAVY* on the leg in big blue letters and a t-shirt. I on the other hand, look like shit in a pair of black leggings and an oversized sweatshirt. Ironically, the one that matches the pants Wes is wearing.

"Yeah," I whisper. "I just didn't know where else to go."

"To me," he says. "When in doubt, you always come home to me and I promise I'll be there to help you sort through it."

"Okay," I agree because that sounds really nice. Wes is my partner in all things and I needed that reminder.

"Let's go home."

Wes wraps his arm around my shoulder and leads me out to my car in the parking lot leaving Lee to sit with Anna in silence. He deposits me into the driver's seat and then I follow him home. Like always, he's waiting in the driveway for me to climb down and then he pulls me gently into the safety of his arms. Wes walks me into the house and up the stairs, down the hall and to our bedroom where he pulls down the covers and tucks me into bed where I fall asleep as best as I can until I need to get up and dress for my best friend's funeral.

What we did not see was Lee sitting with Anna's casket all night until the wee hours of the morning when he left only to shower, shave, and don his dress uniform signifying himself as the Department Captain.

"'Blessed are the Peacemakers for they shall be called the children of God,'" the Pastor invokes the service with after we take our places in the congregation of the Civic Center. The church felt wrong to be the place that we honor Anna's sacrifice at. "While Dr. Anna Garner was not an officer of the law she tended to them. Dr. Garner, I am told, was more a member of this team than she ever realized while here on Earth."

I stand next to Emma, she looks both regal and sad in her simple black wrap dress with lace cap sleeves and heels. Sad, she looks so abundantly sad. My dress uniform is stiff from lack of use. Usually it hangs wrapped in cellophane in the very back of my closet and is only pulled out for tragic events just like this one. Only usually, I stand in the back of the crowd and think what a tragic loss of life or how sad it is to lose a fallen comrade. I'm not sitting in the front section with the other mourners.

For years, I lived fast and loose chasing one case after another with zero regard for my safety. I always thought it would be me who would fall in the line of duty and my parents would stand sad but proud of my bravery. I never once imagined that I would lose someone so integral to my life.

Wes stands beside me looking devastatingly handsome in his black fed suit with a crisp white shirt and black tie. Last night he shined his shoes for hours. Just polishing them over and over again, as though he could never get them shiny enough. Anna would say that was his own way to deal with his grief, so I left him to it but kept a watchful eye just in case he needed me to bring him back from the edge.

"Let us bow our heads and pray," the pastor leads. "Dear Heavenly Father, help us to find solace in you during these dark times. Please guide these officers as they carry their grief for their fallen comrade, their sister in arms." I take the time to listen to his words and think there is nothing that will bring that solace he speaks of. Right now, everything seems so bleak that I can't even fathom a way out of this grief.

After the pastor finishes speaking, Lee dressed immaculately in his uniform, every piece meticulously laid out, steps up to the podium and while he looks perfect, I can see that he is anything but. His lips are pulled tight just so and I can see the whiteness in the corners from strain. His hand shakes just a bit, it's subtle so no one would notice it but me. Or Emma as she stiffens beside me.

"Thank you all for coming," he says. "Anna Garner was an integral part of our Department and while she was not out on patrol tending to the community, she was in the station tending to its officers. This job is not an easy one and she took it on with compassion and grace. It takes a strong person to hear about the things officers see every day and she did with kindness in her heart wanting to ease those burdens and we are all better for having known her."

"Fucking ass," Emma says under her breath.

"Emma," I whisper grabbing her hand in mine. She does not turn to look at me, but she does nod once and then squeeze my hand before dropping our connection.

When Lee steps down from the podium he is replaced on the stage with a choir who sings *Eternal Father*, a staple at all Police and Military funerals.

When the pastor steps up again, "'Blessed are the Peacemakers,' Matthew said," he begins to expound on the passage we all know so well but I can't help but flinch at the name. "Fortunate are we to have those who watch over our community and we are all so fortunate to have them. Jesus knew that those who put their lives on the line for their communities are so special and I would like to touch on that for a moment in the readings of Matthew."

"God, I hate that name," Emma whispers as a shudder wracks through her body causing Lee's attention to focus solely on Emma even though his body does not move and he remains facing forward, I can tell that he is acutely tuned into her.

"I was just thinking the same thing," I whisper back.

When the Mayor steps up to speak I do everything in my power not to roll my eyes. In fact, I'm pretty sure every officer in this building feels the same way. This particular Mayor has never been a big supporter of law enforcement and it shows in his recent budget cuts towards safety equipment like flak jackets and life vests.

"Pompous windbag," I hear Lee mutter under his breath and have to bite my lip to keep from laughing. Laughing at a funeral would be highly inappropriate or so I have been previously told.

All possible outbursts of hilarity are muted when two women from the choir to sing *For Good* from the *Wicked* Soundtrack. It's fitting, and I can't help but cry again. I hate fucking funerals. It's so stupid but as they sing about never seeing one another again and parting ways I can't help but feel like my heart shatters just a little bit more.

"Please welcome, FBI Special Agent in Charge Wesley O'Connell for the tolling of the bells." When Wes is called to the podium to lead the bell ceremony a sob caught in my throat. He looks so handsome in his custom tailored black suit.

"In the Navy, we ring a bell to signify a ship or a sailor lost at sea or in battle. I think it's only fitting that we honor Dr. Anna Garner this way," he explains. "Please join me in a moment of silence as Officer Jones rings the bell twenty-one times in honor of Dr. Anna Parker who I had the extreme pleasure of calling my friend. She will be sorely missed." A sob bubbles up from my throat and Emma reaches for me again.

The bell rings once.

The tears that have burned behind my eyes all morning run freely down my cheeks. I have cried so much that there shouldn't be any tears left to cry.

The bell rings twice.

I'm so fucking angry. How could Anna have been so stupid? Why would she take a risk like that? The gambled with everything and lost.

The bell rings a third time. And then again and again and again until they have rung twenty-one times. Each one like a bullet to my heart.

Wes looks to me and in that moment I mouth the words "Thank you," to him. Thank you for loving me, thank you for this beautiful tribute to our friend, thank you for understanding. He nods once and then exits the stage.

"Color Guard, retire colors," the funeral commander calls out and the uniformed men assigned to the duty pick up their flags and stand in formation at the head of the aisle just in front of Anna's flag cover coffin.

A bagpiper plays *Amazing Grace* as the Color Guard steps forward to make room for the pallbearers. Six more uniformed officers lift up Anna's casket high on their shoulders. We stand in stunned silence as Anna is led out of the Civic Center by the bagpiper followed by the Color Guard and then our own sweet, Anna.

We all file out behind them. Her casket is loaded into a shiny black hearse escorted in the front by three motorcycle patrol and two black and white units in the back with lights flashing. Together she is driven off to the cemetery where she will be buried in a private service in an hour.

We all file into our vehicles marked with bright orange FUNERAL tags and follow soberly behind them. Wes holds my hand as he drives.

We park on the side of the road as Anna's casket is loaded into a horse drawn caisson. And then quietly, our small group walks behind it to end at Anna's final resting place where the pallbearers once again carry her casket from the caisson and then place it on the racks that will eventually lower her into the ground. Every step I take is a step towards the end. Towards goodbye and I feel like there are lead weights in my legs but somehow, I keep moving forward.

"'The Lord is my Shepherd . . .'" the pastor begins to recite Psalm 23 and Wes holds me tight in his arms as I cry freely. There is no stopping them now. Anna is gone, and this is it.

"Please retire colors," the Funeral Commander calls out and I sob as the uniformed officers fold up the flag that had covered the glossy casket and present it to Liam. Lee then turns on his heel and kneels to present the flag to Anna's parents.

"It is with my deepest condolences that I present to you this flag," he says handing it off before stepping back to the side. "And the knowledge that your daughter died bravely in the line of duty."

This is the part that I hate. I know it's coming, we talked about it and everyone felt like it was a fitting final send off to Anna, our one last tradition for a fallen officer but I can already feel myself losing it as Lee turns the dial on the radio that he holds in his hand. Lee clicks the button on the side of the radio three times in quick succession to signify the time was now.

"Dr. Anna Garner . . . this is dispatch paging Dr. Anna Garner . . . Dr. Anna Garner . . ." the radio crackles and another sob bubbles up.

Lee picks up the radio and presses the button on the side. "This is Captain Liam Goodnite of the George Washington Township Police Department. Dr. Anna Garner is officially relieved of duty. End of Watch on this day, the sixth of August."

"Dispatch copies, Captain Goodnite," the voice crackles and I can hear the tears in her voice too. "Dr. Anna Garner is relieved of duty. End of Watch August 6, 2018."

"That concludes our service today," the pastor says. "Immediate friends and family are welcome to stay."

The bulk of this little group peels off, walking back to where the cars were left. There will be a small luncheon provided at the station for all that took duty today and the rest that head back there to go to work. I won't be going. I'm not ready. After this I have a date with my old boyfriends, Jack and Johnny. After that I have no plans.

Together, Wes, Emma, Lee, and I watch as they lower Anna into the ground. It's over. Anna is gone. I wrap my arms around Wes's middle and hold tight until I feel like I can curb the tears.

"You ready to go, baby?" he asks me softly.

"No," I answer. "But I don't think I ever will be."

"Emma—" I hear Lee start.

"Don't," she commands in voice filled with nothing but ice. "Don't you dare."

"Emma, you have to talk to me," he demands.

"No, Lee," she snaps a little wild. "What you don't seem to understand—so I'll say it again louder for the kids in the back—is that I don't have to do anything. The least of which will involve you."

"Emma, I love you," he pleads and it's hard to watch him in this moment of desperation.

"Save it for someone else. You've ruined enough lives here," she spits out with so much venom even I flinch.

"You can't mean that," he says stunned looking like someone hit him.

"I do." And then she walks off never looking back. After she marches out of sight, Lee seems to shake off his shock and chases after her.

"What do we do now?" I turn and ask Wes who is standing just slightly behind me.

He takes my hand and says, "Starting today we put one foot in front of the other and we just go from there. But baby?"

"Yeah?" I answer.

"We go together."

And as we walk out of the cemetery hand in hand I realize that it looks like Emma is falling apart more than I realized. I'm going to have to keep an eye on her and Lee both. But now I feel like I can handle it because I have Wes at my side.

One thing is certain, I was right when I had said everything has changed because it has.

the end . . . for now.

playlist

Praying—Kesha
Love Me Harder—Arianna Grande & The Weeknd
Believer—Imagine Dragons
Him and I—G Eazy and Halsey
Holy Water—Soundgarden
Demons—Imagine Dragons
Pray For Me—The Weeknd Featuring Kendrick Lamar
Savior—Iggy Azalea Featuring Quavo
When You're Gone—the Cranberries
Holy Water—Switchfoot
For Good—Kristin Chenoweth and Idina Menzel
One Foot—Walk the Moon

about jennifer rebecca

Jennifer is a thirty something lover of words, all words: the written, the spoken, the sung (even poorly), the sweet, the funny, and even the four letter variety. She is a native of San Diego, California where she grew up reading the Brownings and Rebecca with her mother and Clifford and the Dog who Glowed in the Dark with her dad, much to her mother's dismay.

Jennifer is a graduate of California State University San Marcos where she studied Criminology and Justice Studies. She is also a member of Alpha Xi Delta.

10 years ago, she was swept off her feet by her very own sailor. Today, they are happily married and the parents of a 9 year old and 7 year old twins. She lives in East Texas where she can often be found on the soccer fields, drawing with her children, or reading. Jennifer is convinced that if she puts her fitbit on one of the dogs, she might finally make her step goals. She loves a great romance, an alpha hero, and lots and lots of laughter.

stalk her

Website
JenniferRebeccaAuthor.com

Newsletter
JenniferRebeccaAuthor.com/Newsletter

Facebook
facebook.com/JenniferRebeccaAuthor

Twitter
@JenniRLreads

Instagram
@JenniRLreads

BookBub
bookbub.com/authors/jennifer-rebecca

Book+Main
bookandmainbites.com/users/22594

Dangerous Dames Facebook Group
facebook.com/groups/JRDangerousDames

also by jennifer rebecca

The Funerals and Obituaries Mysteries
Dead and Buried
Dead and Gone, Coming Summer 2018

The Murder on Ice Mysteries
Attack Zone
Layback, Coming 2019

The Southern Heartbeats Series
Stand (Vol. 1)
Joy (a Southern Heartbeat Holiday), previously featured in then Love, Snow, & Mistletoe Anthology for St. Jude
Whiskey Lullabye (Vol. 2)
Mercy (a Southern Heartbeats Short), free on Wattpad
Just a Dream (Vol. 3), Coming Soon

The Claire Goodnite Thrillers
Tell Me A Story
Tuck Me In Tight
Say A Sweet Prayer
Kiss Me Goodnight

The Wanted Kindle World
Church Bells

VOLUME 4 OF THE claire goodnite SERIES

kiss me goodnight

Coming October 8, 2018

Unedited. Subject to change.

prologue

it's you

THERE IS A MARCHING band pounding away in my brain.

I must have had too much to drink at the rehearsal dinner last night. I think. I can get my ass ready for to-day—*my wedding day*—because if I don't, my bestie, Emma, will have my ass.

I pry my eyes open, only then do I realize that I am not in our hotel room on the coast. I'm not in the luxury king bed full of fluffy pillows and down comforters near a window looking out at the ocean. I'm not where I should be. It takes my brain a minute, still feeling as fuzzy as it is, to realize that I'm not . . . safe.

The light shines through the wooden slats of the doors.

I'm here. I am right back where I started. Where I thought I would die when I was so small, just a baby re-ally. I'm where I once escaped and had naively thought I would never be back. I scoot back on the worn, torn carpet floor of the closet that I was locked in once before, until my back hits the wall. I try to make myself as small as possible hoping against all hope that he won't see me but as I hear the footsteps growing louder and louder, I know that there is no hope to be found at all.

The closet door swings opened and I realize how stupid I have been. All this time that I struggled, that I suffered from those terrible nightmares and prayed that they would either end or I would finally remember just who had tried to harm me when I was just six years old.

All those times I thought I was safe, that I was free, were really nothing but lies because looking down at me with a sinister smile on his face in this little house of horrors from my haunted past is the last person I ever would have thought would be capable of this kind of thing.

The truth is I was never free, I was living under the watchful eye of a monster, a wolf in sheep's clothing just waiting for their chance to pounce. His smile broadens and his eyes glimmer with excitement in the knowledge that he's won.

It's finally over, this game of cat and mouse that we have been silently engaged in for twenty four years.

He pulls his leather belt free from his pants and loops it around my neck. I look up into his warm eyes, ones that I had always trusted as he tightens the leather around my neck.

"It's you. It was always you," I say as suddenly every memory finally clicks into place. Anna would be so proud. I have to tell her when I see her again.

I gasp as the air is squeezed out of my lungs. I struggle to pull more in even though in my brain I know that it isn't possible. Maybe this is how it was always supposed to be. Maybe this is how my story was always supposed to end. My name is Detective Claire Goodnite and I'm about to die.

You know what they say, every story has its ending, I just wish I was prepared for this one. . .

For more information visit:
www.jenniferrebeccaauthor.com/books/kiss-me-goodnite

acknowledgements

I don't know where to start other than thank you, thank you, thank you for picking up this book. You're here with me at book 3 on our way towards the end of this series and to be here you had to have been with Claire and me since the beginning. Thank you for reading this series, for loving Claire and Wes and their story. And also hopefully, thank you for forgiving me for what I put you through in this book. I'll make it better, I promise! Thank you to every lover of my crazy Dames who followed me over to the dark-er side. I promise we'll be back and crazier than ever in 2019!

Thank you to the bloggers who without your kind words of encouragement, I don't know where I would be. Thank you for believing in Claire and me. *HEA Novel Thoughts*, *Dirty Bad*, *Alphas Do It Better*, *Wine Books N' Chill*, *Brittany's Book Blog*, and of course my girls at *Garcia Sisters Book Blog*, not to mention all the other beautiful blogs along the way. I see you, I read every review good or bad, and I take your words to heart. I listen to your advice and hope that along the way I learn from it to be better. Thank you from the bottom of my heart for being on this journey with me.

Thank you to Nazarea Andrews and InkSlinger PR. Happy Anniversary! I cannot believe how far we've come in just a year. I know that with you we can do anything and I am so blessed to have had you all walk into my life. Thank you for your guidance but also your friendship. I cherish both.

Thank you to Lauren for your wonderful support

and friendship. Andrea, thank you for pushing me, for believing in and for being my friend. Jodie, you clumsy kid, thank you for believing in me, for letting me hang with the cool kids and making me feel like I belong. Emma, thank you for your support and guidance. You were the very first person to tell me I had a seat at the table when I published and you will never know just how much that still means to me. Sara, thank you for your friendship and for being so generous with your advice and support. It means the world to me. Thank you for leading me down a dark path of sexy highlanders. I feel like I will never be the same. Thank you for making me feel welcome when I would want to hide in a corner and chew my hair. Not really, but kind of. I love you all and I am so honored to be in your company.

Thank you to Stephanie Atienza of Uplifting Design for making the words that come out of my head make sense. It's not easy for someone with dysgraphia and dyslexia to put their words to paper. Sometimes it's amazing, sometimes it's so jumbled I'm not even sure what I meant. Thank you for straightening me out on paper and in life. Thank you for your unwavering friendship of 15 years. Thank you for being a bright spot in both happy days and hard. For hard truths and also encouragement when I need both or either.

Thank you to Alyssa Garcia of Uplifting Designs for the gorgeous cover and formats. What a wild ride this has been, huh? Did you ever think we would be wrapping up a successful series? That people would want to read my words? Because I never thought any of this was a possibility. I would still be writing late at night and hiding my words, afraid to show anyone if you hadn't walked into my life and taken charge. You're the structure to my crazy and my very favorite travel buddy. Thank you for believing in me before I even did. Thank you for your unwavering loyalty and support, but also for your friendship. You're stuck now so congratulations. :/

Thank you to my mom and dad who love and support me through this craziness. Thank you for helping with baseball and gymnastics and soccer. And all that freaking common core math I'm not smart enough to do. Thank you for not letting me quit even when I wanted to. I hope in all of this, I have made you proud.

And last, but never least, my handsome guy. Sean, I couldn't do this without you and even if I could, I wouldn't want to. It's always been you and me against the world and that's how I want to spend the rest of my life. Life with you has never been a challenge. I give you crap for your underwear on the towel rack, but really, my life is beautiful. Thank you for that. Thank you for how hard your work for the kids and I and how much you love us. It takes a strong man to be a great husband and father and baby, you're the best. So much so that there is a piece of you in every badass alpha and every happily ever after I write. You've left your mark on every part of my world and also my heart. Happy Anniversary. The best thing I did was walk into that party because every since then, it's been only you I see. It's only ever been you.